~*Heaven's Sinners*~

Heaven's Sinners

Copyright © 2013 Bella Jewel

Heaven's Sinners is a work of fiction. All names, characters, places and events portrayed in this book either are from the author's imagination or are used fictitiously. Any similarity to real persons, living or dead, establishments, events, or location is purely coincidental and not intended by the author. Please do not take offence to the content, as it is FICTION.

~*ACKNOWLEDGEMENTS*~

There are so many people I would like to thank, it's quite possible I could take up two pages with it. The support I have received with writing these books, has been utterly mind blowing. I've had so many kind people offering to help, from blogs, to fans, to people I don't even know. You're all amazing, each and every one of you. Now, to the personal thanks.

To Lola Stark – my snatch grabber. She's my budgie eating, whale toe, crazy friend who kept me smiling throughout this book. Without her, and her hilarious voxer messages, I think I would have given up many times. You're my crazy bitch until the end of time snatch grab, and you know it!

To Sali Benbow-Powers – my crazy, enthusiastic reader. Your notes kept me going, you ripped a smile out of me every time, without a doubt. Your personality is like a breath of fresh air, as I've told you before. You're the kind of girl people go to when they're feeling down, because you're bound to make them smile! You know you rocked my book, so you know, I'll rock you back!

To Lauren Mckellar, for editing this book for me. You took the time out, chatted with me the entire way, and were so sweet about it. You're utterly amazing, and I feel so lucky to have snatched you up. No doubt there are many out there who would like to grab you and keep you. But they can't, you're mine, Muahahahaha!!

To Ari from Coverit Designs. Girl, you rock my covers. Seriously, you're the best cover artist ever. You just get an idea, and you make it amazing. Without you, this book wouldn't look pretty, which means no one would buy it, so girl, you get half the damn credit!! I love your work!

To Love Between The Sheets for an AMAZING cover reveal tour, blog tour and all the other tours you took the time out to help me with. You ladies got my name out there, you helped me grow and expand. I can't wait to do a blog tour with you, your energy is addictive!

To Totally Booked, for giving me a chance. You ladies were so friendly, warm and inviting. You shared my teasers and gave me one hell of a goodreads TBR list! Thanks to you, half of Facebook is now sure to know my name. Rock on and keep doing what you do best!

To Wendy Bragg Yoder for reading my book, and going through and picking out all those tiny things we missed. You are amazing, and seriously you fix everything. I adore you. Thank you.

And of course to all my fans – You know without all of you, this wouldn't be possible. So to each and every one of you reading this right now, THANK YOU!! Keep doin' what you do best, and that's reading!!

~*LINKS*~

You can find me on Facebook and keep up to date with all my future releases.

Author Bella Jewel

Bella Jewel

If the above links don't work, just jump on Facebook and type in my name, that should work. (Under **AUTHOR BELLA JEWEL**)

~*BOOKS IN THIS SERIES*~

Hell's Knights - Available on amazon now. Purchase Here

Heaven's Sinners (You are reading it now)

Knights Sinner (Jackson's story, release date TBA)

PROLOGUE

PAST - SPIKE

Red.

Most people love the color red - it's sexy, alluring, and beautiful. A woman in red can take your breath away, and make your entire world stop. A red car makes your blood start pumping and adrenalin course through your veins. A red rose, indicates love and commitment. Red lips can steal your heart. Red, in the big scheme of things, indicates pure beauty. Until you see it in its darkest form.

Blood.

Suddenly, red no longer represents beauty, fun, and living; instead it represents death, pain, agony and heartbreak. When faced with it in that form, it's heart wrenching, horrible, brutal and life changing.

I see the color red every time I close my eyes, I see it every time I look at a car, I see it every time I think of her...my wife. Red consumes me. It takes me to a place I struggle to escape from. Red fills me with the one emotion I can't ever remove from my heart.

Guilt.

CHAPTER 1

PRESENT - SPIKE

I wake up panting, my entire body shakes and sweat rolls down my cheeks. I can taste a mild salty flavor in my mouth, and I realize I've been screaming - again. Some people would see a man screaming as a sign of weakness. It's just human nature. Men who scream, cry, or feel too much emotion, are pussies, end of fucking story. I only scream when I sleep, and each morning I wake up feeling the same - alone, cold, empty, and riddled with guilt. I've learned to live with the fact that I'll never feel any different, that my life will always be lived in a pit of fuckin' darkness.

That's what I deserve.

Sliding out of bed, I take hold of my sheets, and pull, taking them with me. I walk out of the room; my chest is still rising and falling heavily. I stop by the washing machine and drop the sheets in, before continuing into the living room. The place is dark, not a light to be seen.

It's early, probably 3 am. It always happens in the morning, like I'm being fuckin' punished. Like sleeping is taking me away from the guilt for a few hours, and that's just not allowed. It's almost as if I'm being forced to live with it, every waking minute of my fucking dark, damaged life.

I fumble for the lights, and when I finally get my finger on one, I flick it. When the room is lit up, I walk towards the kitchen. The house is only small, but I'm not planning on being around for long. I need to organize a few things, and then I'll be on my way. This is the Knights grounds, it ain't mine. Me and my club have to move on eventually. The only reason we're hangin' around now is because

Jackson has a fuckin' soft spot for me. Christ knows why. He should have wiped his hands of me long ago.

Thinking about the club has my head spinning. Once, a long time ago, Jackson asked me to be part of the Hell's Knights. I thought about it too, and was planning on saying yes, but life took me in another direction. Drugs took over, I got myself tangled in some bad shit, and then I lost my wife.

After that, I bolted. I fucked random women, I drank a lot, I smoked a lot, and then I decided to create my own MC club. That's where the Sinner's came in to play. Since then, I've been preparing to end the bad shit once and for all, starting with the drug lord who killed my wife.

He won't like what's comin' for him.

It ain't gonna be pretty when it goes down. It's going to be a blood bath, and chances are I won't come out alive. Don't fuckin' care either. Just gotta end it. That's all I know. It's all I breathe for. It's life for me right now.

I grip a coffee cup, running my fingers around the faded rim. I'm just about to put it under the old, fucked up machine when my cell rings. Staring down at the ID, I see it's my VP, Granger. With a curse, I pick up the phone and put it to my ear. What the fuck is he doing, calling me this early for?

"What?" I bark.

"Yo' Spike, got a bit of an issue down here at the bar."

Fuckin' hell, if it's not one thing, it's another.

"What's goin' down? Better be fuckin' important, Granger."

"That girl that came to the warehouse last month. You know, the pretty one?"

Ciara. Just thinkin' about her makes my skin tingle. I'm still not sure if it's a good or bad thing. She's gettin' to me, creepin' into my thoughts and refusing to move. I don't know why the girl is so determined to get to me. Why she can't just let it go. She needs to let it go, god knows the girl is better off without me. She always was. She just couldn't see it. She always saw beauty when all I saw was ugly. She's that kind of person. She sees the light in everyone.

"Ciara," I growl into the phone. "And she ain't my problem, so why the fuck are you callin' me?"

"Well, her and the other girl, Cade's Old Lady, are a bit under the weather and are bein' harassed by a few men. It's gettin' a bit ugly, but the stubborn ass bitch won't leave."

"Addison is Cade's fuckin' problem, she ain't mine."

Addison is Cade's Old Lady and a royal pain in my ass - a pain that I'm kind of getting used to, though I won't tell her that. Damn woman is addictive as fuck, and she knows how to get under a man's skin with all her 'let's be friends' bullshit. Like I said, pain in my ass.

"Called Cade, he's comin' for her. Ciara is refusin' to leave with him sayin' it's her bar and she's not gettin' run outta it. I say Cade's gonna have enough trouble gettin' the other one out, let alone two. So, I called you."

Fuck. Fuck. Fuck. Ciara is not who I want to see right now. She winds me up the wrong way, and she brings out too much shit inside me that I really don't wanna deal with right now, or ever, for that matter.

"Fine, I'm fuckin' comin'. Get the bitch outside and hold her there, yeah?"

"On it."

I slam the phone closed and spin around, storming toward the door. I grip a pair of jeans, yanking them up and over my legs, and then I throw on an old, black shirt. I grip my bike keys, my helmet and then I'm out the door. Fuckin' hell. Why am I even doing this? Ciara and I don't get along, the whole world knows that, and yet here I am, going to save her fuckin' ass. I'm doing it for Cheyenne; she would want me to make sure Ciara is safe.

Yeah fucking right.

Who am I trying to fool?

~*~*~*~

PRESENT - CIARA

"Addi is no whore!" I yell, hurling the pool cue at a random skinny man, who has decided to start an argument with us.

"Fuckin' throw that at me once more, bitch, and I'll knock you the fuck out!"

Addi storms towards him, fists balled, dark hair swinging. Just before she reaches him, one of Spike's minions grips her and tosses her backwards. She crashes into me and we both stumble into the bar. Ouch, dammit, that hurt. I shoot the biker an angry glare, which he returns with full force.

"You two fuckin' sit and wait for your rides," he growls.

He's frustrated. He's been trying to get us outside for the past ten minutes, with no luck. I'm sure he'd just love to throw us over his shoulder and toss us out, but he's not about to risk that in a bar with this many people - biker or not.

I cross my arms. "You can't make us sit here, dude."

Addi turns, giving me a broad grin. "Did you just call him dude?"

I throw my head back and laugh, and soon she's joining in. The angry biker storms over, grips my arm and shakes me harshly. My teeth clatter, and my head spins just a touch. Bloody tequila shots.

"Fuckin' hell, shut your damn mouth, girl. You two are gonna end up on your asses in a minute."

"Tell your whores to shut their mouths!" an angry man from the back of the bar yells.

The biker turns, and gives him a truly fowl glare. "You better watch your fuckin' mouth, or I'll come over there and ram that pool cue up your motherfuckin' ass."

Addi gives me a look, but behind it I can see she's completely amused. She came down tonight...well...last night, technically, considering it's morning now, to have a few drinks with me after my shift.

I recently started working here, trying to get myself a little more money so I could save enough to go to college. My parents don't know I'm here. I left after Chey died, in an attempt to escape their wallowing. It got to a point where neither of them smiled anymore, or laughed, or joked, or even held me. Cheyenne was the golden child, and somehow it turned into being my fault she'd died, because I was the one who befriended Spike in the first place.

12

"Uh-oh, we've got company and he doesn't look happy," Addison whispers into my ear.

I turn and follow the direction of her eyes to see Spike entering the bar. He's furious, and his body language screams anger. His eyes are wild, his fists clenched, his chest heaving and his body rigid. Damn, he looks so gorgeous. He's like sex on legs. He's *that* kind of beautiful. His sandy blonde hair is messy, like he's just rolled out of bed. His brown eyes almost look black from this distance. His dark shirt is stretched across his chest, showing off muscles I know are toned, hard and...well...sexy as fuck. His old faded jeans ride low on his hips, and his black boots are unlaced. He looks as though he wants to deck someone.

His eyes scan the crowd then fall on me and Addi. Being the typical smart-ass she is, Addi lifts her hand and waves, calling out, "Hey friend!"

Spike gives her a glare, and begins storming over. I actually take a step back. He's quite intimidating when he wants to be - I should know, I've taken him on during some of his worst moods. He's just about near Addison and I when the tall lanky guy yells out a string of rude, vulgar words. Spike stops, stiffens, and then spins around quickly. Suddenly, he's charging toward the guy, fists balled and ready for action. The biker who was trying to get us outside lunges at him, but misses by just a few millimeters. Spike raises his fist and hits lanky guy in the face, sending him flying across the bar.

Glasses smash, girls scream, and suddenly, men are everywhere. Fists are flying, chairs are being broken and bottles are being smashed over people's heads. Addi yelps, and takes hold of my hand, pulling me backwards. I stare, wide-eyed, as men group up and beat the living shit out of each other. Why do they do that? Someone throws a punch and suddenly they're all in it, beating each other senseless.

13

Addi and I duck around a corner, just as a bottle comes soaring past our heads. It smashes against the wall, and I flinch. Shit. I didn't mean to cause an all-out brawl, that wasn't my intention…it was just a little fun.

"CIARA!"

I hear Spike's booming voice, and I jerk. Shit, he's going to abuse the hell out of me for this. I tug Addi into the dark hall, lit only by faded, yellow lights. I hear Spike bellow my name again, so I pull Addi back even further. I really do not want to take Spike on when he's in this kind of mood. He's not pretty when he's like this.

Addi leans in close, whispering into my ear. "He's going to find you honey, you better go out."

"He's going to kill me," I snap back, my voice barely above a whisper.

She nods, lifting her hair into her hands and tying it up. "Join the club. Cade is going to flip when he arrives."

"Ciara, get your motherfuckin' ass out here, *NOW!*"

Shit. Dammit. I give Addi a worried stare. At least Cade will go easy on her. Spike is far different. Spike doesn't take people's shit. At all. Ever.

"He won't hurt you, honey."

"He's pissed, he sure as shit won't be nice about it. He hates me."

She shakes her head, giving me a comforting expression. "He doesn't hate you, or he wouldn't be here."

14

"He's here because he feels guilty…like he has to be here for the sake of Chey. I'm a pity case. He wouldn't have come otherwise."

Addi gives me a look, and crosses her arms. "That's not true, and you know it. He's going to get hold of you, so you might as well get your cute ass out there and face him."

"Or," I say, turning and hurrying toward the back entrance, "I could go out here and…"

"You fuckin' take one more step toward that door, and I'll fuckin' drop you, Ciara."

Stiffening at the icy voice, I slowly turn to see Spike standing at the end of the hall. He's panting, bloody and wild with anger. *Oh shit*. Addi even takes a step back, which is odd for her, because she's usually cocky around Spike.

"Addison, get your fuckin' ass out front now. Your man is lookin' for you, and he ain't happy. Don't even fuckin' dare to open those pretty lips and smart mouth me."

Addi turns, giving me a sorry expression. "I gotta go, call me," she whispers.

"Addison!" I yell, but she's already hurrying past Spike and out into the bar.

I stand at the end of the hall, staring at the angry biker in front of me. Seriously, part of me is still contemplating turning and running. It's not a bad plan, considering how angry Spike is right now. His eyes are flaring, his lips tight…he's mega pissed. Sure, I know I deserve it, but it doesn't mean I'm going to go willingly. I lift my foot and take a step backwards, and I can see him visibly stiffen.

15

His brown eyes flash with anger, and his jaw ticks. Shit. He's gone far and beyond pissed.

"I'm not fucking with you, Ciara. You fuckin' take one step, and I'll put you over my motherfuckin' shoulder. You turn around, get over here, and do as you're fuckin' told."

Not going to happen. I spin quickly, and run toward the door. I manage to get to it, out of it, and halfway across the car lot before he gets hold of me. His fingers curl around my arm and he hauls me backwards, so hard that I slam into his body. His arm goes down and wraps around my waist, pressing my back to his chest. His other arm releases mine, and moves up and over my chest. He's got me fully secured now, and even with my best squirming efforts, I can hardly move.

"Are you fuckin' stupid? Didn't anyone teach you not to piss off an already pissed off biker?" he growls into my ear.

"Didn't anyone ever teach you not to manhandle a woman?" I cry, struggling in his grips.

"Ain't no woman here."

"Fuck you, Spike."

"Been there, done that, wasn't memorable."

That asshole. I lift my leg and shove it backwards, right into his knee. He bellows and lets me go, and I lurch forward. Lunging towards me, he catches my ankle and I fall, hard.

I land on my stomach, arms out in front of me, face centimeters from the dirt. He keeps hold of my ankle as I thrash and try to kick him enough to make him let go. Grunting, he crawls up my body, flattening his over mine. I shudder. I'm ashamed that I do, because right now I want to punch him, but it happens. A ripple of life runs through my body at the feeling of his hard, sexy body pressing against my back. I won't lie; I've wanted to fuck Spike again since the day he took my virginity, but there's no way I'd swallow my pride and admit that to him now.

He leans down so he's close to my ear, his breath hot against it. "We're goin' to get up, walk toward my bike, get on it and leave. If you try and run, I'll fuckin' knock you out and throw you on unconscious."

He probably would too. Asshole.

"I'm not going anywhere with you," I spit, squirming.

"Yeah, you are. Can argue all fuckin' morning about it, or you can get up, get on my bike and I can take you home."

"Why are you even here?" I growl. "You hate me."

"Coz' there ain't no other fucker wantin' to save your ass."

That hurts, because he's right. No one else would want to save my ass. Not one person except him, and he doesn't even like me. That says a lot about my life.

"Fine," I whisper, my voice having lost its spark. "Just take me home."

He lifts his body off mine, and I feel his muscles moving against my back. Dammit. I manage to push myself up on my hands and knees, groaning as I do. I hear a distinct hiss, and it takes me a moment to realize it's because I'm on my knees, flashing my ass at him, and I'm wearing nothing more than a G-string under a short skirt. I quickly push myself into a kneeling position. My cheeks flush red, and I don't dare to turn and see his expression. He's

17

probably disgusted. His precious Cheyenne would have never worn something so…so…trashy. I peer down at my knees and see there's dots of blood all over them.

"You gave me bloody knees, you jerk-off."

He snorts, and I turn to look at him. He's staring down at me, looking so completely breathtaking, it's almost blinding. His arms are crossed, and his jeans have patches of dirt covering them. Fuck him for being so beautiful. It should be illegal.

"You gave me no choice," he grinds out. "Now get up."

I get to my feet, and dust myself off.

"Don't know what my sister ever saw in you, chauvinistic pig," I mumble under my breath.

"Say it out loud, Ciara. It won't be nothin' you haven't fuckin' spat at me before."

I lift my head and glare at him. "Just take me home."

"With fuckin' pleasure."

I turn, and begin walking toward his bike. I know Spike's bike, I've seen him getting around on it. It's similar to the one we used to ride together, back when he actually liked me. That was a time I think about often. Before Chey decided she wanted him, Spike and I were great friends. Up until the night he fucked me to get to my sister.

I lift the helmet off the seat, and pull it down over my head. Spike grips his, doing the same before climbing onto the seat and starting the 105th Anniversary, Black and Gold, Softail Deluxe. It's a beautiful bike. I climb onto the back, and put my hands on my knees. With a growl, Spike reaches back, gripping my fingers and pulling them around his waist. As soon as he lets them go, I quickly pull them back.

"I know how to be a passenger on a bike, Spike. *You* were the one who taught me how to sit, and not have to hold on."

He exhales loudly and angrily, before reaching back for my hands. I lift them in the air.

"For fucks sake, Ciara. Give me your fuckin' hands. I'm not in the mood to fuck around with you. I know I taught you how to hold on, but you haven't been on a fuckin' bike in years."

Dammit, he's right. Sighing in defeat, I put my hands on his sides, tangling my fingers through the belt loop holes on his faded jeans.

He walks the bike out of the parking spot, and then starts it, pulling the throttle and sending it forward. When his boots are up on the pegs, I relax a little. I've always hated the taking off part - call me paranoid.

Spike pulls out onto the highway, and picks up speed. The wind is cool against my face, and I close my eyes, breathing it in. I've always loved being on the back of his bike, we used to do it all the time. He used to pick me up each day for work and together we'd ride around, hanging out, just doing what friends do.

Then Cheyenne came into the picture.

Spike takes me to my tiny apartment, and it surprises me that he knows where it is. He stops in the driveway, and turns the bike off.

My heart begins to pound because I'm tired of all the fighting, and yet I can't see it stopping anytime soon. I don't want any more of it tonight. Maybe I should just walk inside, shut the door in his face and lock it. Yeah right - I know as well as he does, that won't happen. I'm too nice. That's what I've been told anyway. I can't turn people away. I'm always trying to fix things. That's what you get, for trying to be a good person.

"You're bleedin'," Spike says simply after we're both off the bike.

I glance down at my knees. The blood is running down my legs now, and over my toes. Super.

"It's fine, I'll sort it."

"My fault," he grunts. "I'll fix it."

I look up, and for a moment our eyes meet and I see something else behind his hard, angry expression. Maybe it's a speck of the boy I used to adore so much.

"It's fine," I whisper. "We both know you don't really want to help me."

"Don't fuckin' tell me how I feel."

"You told me to go and die last month," I point out, crossing my arms.

He flinches. "I was fuckin' mad that you came back tryin' to get my forgiveness."

"Yeah, well, I'm fuckin' mad that you're here trying to help me when you've done nothing but treat me like shit for years."

His eyes widen. I'm not really sure if it's because I swore in the same tone he did, or if my words actually surprise him.

"Never made false promises to you, Ciara."

My mouth drops open. "Are you serious?" I cry. "Don't pretend you didn't know how I felt about you, Spike. We were the best of friends, and you knew I had feelings there, yet you still chose to use me to get to my sister. Don't stand here and pretend you didn't know what you were doing. You fucked me, you took my virginity, all to get back at her."

His eyes scan my face a moment, then he shoves his hands in his pockets.

"You wanted that fuck, Ciara. You wanted me to fuck you from the minute you turned eighteen."

I'm shaking now. "I wanted you to *feel* it, that's what I wanted. I wanted, no, I *needed* to be more than just a revenge fuck and yet that's all I was. You came up to me that night, you made me feel like a fucking queen and all along, it was you just seeking out a way to make Cheyenne pay. I didn't expect you to care about me, Spike, because clearly you didn't, but I did expect that you would have respected me more than that, being that you were my friend," I stop speaking, and run a shaky hand through my hair. "I thought I meant a little more to you, but I was wrong. You hurt me. You fucked me on my first time, when you should have made love. If you couldn't have done that, you should have never come for me. You could have gone and got your revenge with some dirty slut, but no, you chose to rip my virginity from me by making me think you cared…"

He jerks at my words, and for a moment, his hand moves as if he wants to reach for me, but he quickly drops it.

"It wasn't…"

"Don't bother. I don't want to hear it. I've heard enough… I heard enough when you whispered sweet nothings in my ear. It

21

doesn't matter in the end. You and Cheyenne deserved each other because you were both fake and selfish."

He growls now. "Don't talk about her like that!"

"Why not?" I scream. "Why can't I talk about your precious wife like that? She was the sunshine in everyone's lives. She was the perfect daughter, the perfect wife, the perfect god damned sister and what was I? Nothing more than a thorn in all of your sides. I never compared, I never even came close. She lapped it up, every fucking second of it. She had you all wrapped around her finger and she knew it. She didn't even want you, Spike, she only did it because I wanted you. She always had to have what I wanted. Screw you, I hate you as much as I fucking hate her!"

Tears are streaming down my face now and I spin, rushing toward my front door. He never should have gotten that much emotion from me. He doesn't deserve it.

My words were unfair, and a big part of me knows that. To Spike, Cheyenne was the prefect wife. She adored him. She treated him well. She was sweet and kind. To me, she was my sister, and I loved her, but I also knew what she was like deep down. Spike was never the man she wanted for herself. She had feelings for him, and yes, she grew to love him, but it was only because of me that she began to look in the first place.

"Ciara, don't fuckin' walk away…"

I spin around. "Fuck you. I never said that to you, and I should have. I've been all over the place with this. For the longest time, I blamed you for her death, but that was my hurt coming out over you, it wasn't because of fact. When I realized it was unfair and it wasn't your fault, I came back and tried to make it better. I tried to make it better for the man who was once my friend, but you shot me down.

So I'm saying what should have been said, from the very moment you started using me to get to her. Fuck you, Danny!"

We're both quiet for a long moment, eyes meeting, hearts pounding. It's him that speaks.

"I might deserve that, but I wasn't the only one who fucked up."

I glare at him. "No, you weren't. That's the problem. I know I fucked up too, but I'm trying, Spike. I'm trying to fix what I broke."

"Ain't nothin' to be fixed. I was done with you years ago, and nothin' you can do will ever get that back. You need to get that in your head, and leave it there, Ciara."

"You know what's so pathetic about this situation?" I rasp, my hands shaking. "It's that no matter how angry I am at you, no matter how many times you spit hurtful words at me, or how many times I keep telling myself to walk away, I can't. I want to save you. I want that friend that I know is in there. I can't walk away, Spike. I hate you, and yet I can't walk away."

His eyes are full of anger and pain when he spits out his next words. "Don't want you to fuckin' save me, Ciara. Don't want you in my fuckin' life. When will you get that through your head? I don't want to be in your life. I didn't chose *you*, I chose *her*. You need to fuckin' move on. I am not the same person I was before."

I laugh, even though hot tears are running down my cheeks. I won't let him break me now. Not after everything I've fought for. His words burn, they wrap around my heart and squeeze so tightly I struggle to breathe.

"See, that's where you're wrong. I know that person is in there, and I won't stop until I find something inside you worth believing in again.

"So keep trying, Spike. You can spit hateful words at me as much as you want. You might have given up on the friendship we built all those years ago, but I didn't. I never did, and as much as you hate it, I *never* will."

Then I spin, and I walk inside before he can say another word. Spike needs to know someone isn't going to give up on him. He needs to know someone is willing to fight. My head is screaming at me to turn him away and run, but my heart is telling me to stay and fight for what I believe in.

And I believe in him.

Somewhere inside, I know he's still there.

CHAPTER 2

PRESENT - CIARA

I stand at the door for long moments, wiping my eyes and gathering myself. I hear his Harley start up, and speed off. With a deep breath, I turn, and make my way into the kitchen. Just as I reach the counter, my phone rings. Sighing, I look down and see Addi's name flashing on the screen. I bet she got in big trouble for our behavior tonight. We were only having fun, but when you're dating a biker, you don't do that kind of thing. Not without your man by your side, anyway. Cade trusts her, and he's fairly easygoing when it comes to letting her go out, but Addi has far too much spunk for her own good and ends up in trouble more often than not.

"Hey," I say, trying to make my voice sound reasonably normal.

"Hey honey, are you ok?"

"I should be asking the same thing…"

She laughs softly. "Yeah, I'm ok. Make-up sex fixes everything."

"Ah," I cry. "*TMI*, Addi!"

She giggles. "Yeah, well, it keeps him calm. Speaking of, how did you and Spike end the night? You weren't removing anything…were you?"

Addi knows about Spike's little fetishes. Having a woman remove his piercings is one of them.

When he was with me, I didn't get a chance to do it. He took them out himself. Well, actually, he didn't take them out as such - he

25

just removed the spikes. They are these little spikey ends that slide over the ends of the barbells. Still, he enjoys making a woman pull them off…with her mouth…so I've heard.

I snort. "No, that did *not* happen. I care about myself far more. He dropped me off, and left. It was fine," I lie.

"Well, now I know you're lying because I can hear you've been crying."

"Damn you, Addi."

She chuckles again. "Well, I rang to give you a heads up. Another angry, over-protective biker is about to pull up in your driveway."

"What? Who?"

"Cade."

"Aw, Addi, did you send Cade over?" I groan.

"He's angry at you, but mostly he's worried because you left with Spike. I couldn't stop him, you know what he's like. He's known you as long as Spike has, he cares about you."

I grumble under my breath, "Damn bikers."

Addi snorts. "Yeah, you got that right. I'm going to bed now, my head's beginning to hurt…stupid shots. I'll call you tomorrow, ok?"

"Yeah, thanks babe."

I hang up the phone and sigh. Cade, great, just what I need. Another big, bad, biker lecture. I'm grateful it's going to come from Cade, though. He's always been the nicest towards me, Jackson coming in at a close second. Addi is very lucky to have them both in

26

her life. They'd die a million times over for her. She had a rough life, and is only just coming good after a very recent kidnapping that nearly ended badly for her. Since then, her and Cade have been inseparable, and I can understand why. It scared the life out of him when she was taken. Jackson too. I am glad to have found a friend in Addi, over the past weeks we have gotten closer. It's nice to have someone.

I hear the rumble of the Harley-Davidson long before it pulls into my drive. Sighing, I quickly pull on some pajama bottoms and slip on an old, baggy shirt. Cade really doesn't need to see me in my tiniest skirt. I hear the sound of his boots crunching up the path, and then I hear his fist banging on the door. Bikers; they never do anything quietly. I stand there for a moment, contemplating whether to let him in or pretend I'm asleep. Mean, I know, but Cade always overreacts. I don't know if I can deal with anymore flaw pointing tonight.

"Open up, Tom Cat. Know you're in there."

Well, at least he's calling me Tom Cat. That has to mean something, right?

I walk over, and open the front door. Cade is standing there, dark jeans, leather jacket, looking like the biker version of a model. He's beautiful. Inky black hair, light eyes, olive skin, tatts everywhere. Cade is what most women dream about.

I can't help but smile when I see his serious expression. Cade and I have always been close, so it doesn't scare me when he tries that one on.

"Don't smirk at me girl, you know you're in deep shit."

I raise my eyebrows and block the doorway as he goes to step in.

27

"How come I'm the one getting yelled at, and Addi is home sleeping? Is it because I can't offer make-up sex?"

His lips twitch, but he doesn't crack a smile. "Addi got her ass slapped for what she did, don't you fuckin' worry about that. Now, it's your turn, minus the ass slapping. You gonna let me in?"

"If I say no..."

He leans forward, grips my shoulders and lifts, moving me out of the way—then he steps through the door. I roll my eyes, and turn, walking into the kitchen. I hear Cade following, and I can't wait for the lecture I'm about to get...really...I can't wait.

"What's goin' on with you, Tom Cat?"

Here we go.

"Nothing," I say, opening the fridge and pulling out a bottle of water.

"Don't fuckin' bullshit me. You came to town after your sister died, we let you lean on us until you found a job, then you got a job, found a place and things were goin' well for you...until Spike came into town. Then you went off the rails. You snuck my woman to his compound..."

"Hey!" I snap, cutting him off and spinning around to face him. "She wanted to go there, not me!"

"Either way, it ain't like you. Then tonight...what the fuck was goin' down in your head?"

"I was having fun, Cade."

"No, you were bein' a shit stirrer."

I cross my arms, and he does too, giving me a hard expression.

28

"What's it to you, anyway?"

He raises his brows. "Are you fuckin' stupid? I've been friends with you for a long time, Ciara, and you matter. Anyone who matters to me, I protect. You went out tonight lookin' for a brawl."

"No, I was having a few drinks with Addi, and it got out of hand."

"You don't do that shit. You are the one who walks away…"

"Yeah," I bark. "Well maybe I'm sick of being who I am. Look where it got me…"

He uncrosses his arms and steps forward. I step back. "Now we're getting somewhere."

"Look, Cade, you know I respect you, but I'm not going to discuss this any further. I don't owe anybody an explanation for what I'm doing. If you want to be angry at Addi, go right ahead, but it has nothing to do with me."

"Do you think that shit speech is actually going to stop me from protectin' you?"

"It should!" I growl.

"Well it doesn't. Stop pushing the ones that care away, Tom Cat."

"I'm doing nothing! I'm just living, Cade. Same way you are."

"Not the same as I am! You're fighting to fix something that can't be fixed. You need to let go of this shit with Spike. It ain't doin' you any favors."

"This has nothing to do with Spike."

"It has everything to do with Spike, and you know it. He ain't worth this sort of pain, Tom Cat. He ain't worth the fight. He's fucked up, he needs to deal with his shit before anyone attempts to make a decent man out of him."

"When did you stop believing in him?" I whisper.

Cade flinches. "I didn't."

"You did, because the way you just spoke about him tells me you don't think he can be fixed. I think you're wrong, Cade. I think Spike is broken, but I also think he can be put back together."

"Maybe he can, but it ain't from you, sugar."

"Because I'm not good enough…" I mumble.

"Stop that shit," he barks, stepping closer and giving me a fierce glare. "You're too good for him, that's the fuckin' problem. Spike is gonna hurt you, just because he can. Don't be the one in his firing line."

"I'm not in his firing line. Hell Cade, he can't even see me."

Cade tilts his head to the side. "You love him still, don't you? It's why you're actin' out."

"No. I despise him."

Cade snorts. "Okay, Tom Cat. Let me tell you something anyway, just for the fuckin' sake of it, because clearly there's so much more I can't see. I don't owe Spike anything, but I do owe you plenty, so here goes. Spike wanted you, before Chey came into the picture. Before everything went south, Spike had feelings for you. They went pretty deep. Do you think he would pick just anyone up and take them to work every day? I can tell you he wouldn't. He was tryin' and you were just seein' him as a friend - all those years, and

30

you friend-zoned him. He figured you wanted nothin' more than that, so he moved on. He saw Chey, he fell for her and she became his obsession. What he did to you, it was fucked up, but it wasn't just a revenge fuck, Tom Cat. Part of Spike wanted that...and then you ran...and you know how it ended."

"You're wrong," I rasp.

My entire body is shaking, and I'm gripping onto the counter for dear life. Cade's wrong. Spike would have told me if he cared about me. He saw my sister and from there forward, he didn't look back. He never made a move on me, aside from the night we slept together. Cade's wrong. He's wrong. He is.

"He would have told me," I whisper, feeling my eyes sting with unshed tears.

"Spike's a fuckin' hard man. He doesn't throw himself at anyone, Tom Cat. You two were friends, but you always kept your distance. That told him you didn't want him. Chey came along, and she threw herself at him. She went out of her way to get his attention and so he went with her, because he thought there was nothing between you two. He went on to fall in love with Chey. She was his first love, and she changed something inside of him, but Tom Cat, she isn't who he wanted to begin with."

"You're saying...because I didn't throw myself at him the way my sister did...that I missed out?"

Cade shrugs, but it's gentle. "Sorry Tom Cat, but that's just how Spike works. He's not the type to chase women, he never has been. Chey made it easy for him, it's the only reason he looked."

"He looked," I grind out, "because they all did. Chey had that effect on men. She was sunshine, and me..."

31

"Don't," he growls. "Don't fuckin' say anything about yourself. Spike thought you were the damned prettiest thing he'd seen in years, he spoke about you all the time."

"How do you know all this?" I snap, trying my best to cover the emotions eating away at each other inside of me.

"Coz' one night, a few months before she died, they had a fight. Spike came over, and he spat out a lot to me. He grumbled on about picking the wrong sister. We got talkin' about it, and that's when he told me he had feelings for you before Chey came along. He said it was your eyes, they used to get him every time…"

I snort. "That's such a typical line."

"Tom Cat, you have wicked sweet eyes."

I look away. "What kind of biker says wicked sweet?"

Cade laughs. "This one. Hey, turn your eyes here, yeah?"

I look back at him, and try to hide my trembling lip. "He never even said sorry for what he did. I ran, and when I came back they were married. He never tried to find me…never tried to contact me. Then when Chey died, he just hated me and I don't know why."

"You do know why," Cade says, his voice suddenly hard for his friend.

"No, I don't."

"Sugar, *yeah*, you do. You and Spike were friends for a long time. He fucked up, and you ran. You never said goodbye, you never even had it out with him. He never heard from you, he couldn't find you, and so he went on and did what he did with Chey. Then, she died and he sees you again…after all those years, and what did you do?"

My heart begins hammering against my chest, and my throat constricts painfully. "I blamed him."

"Yeah, you did. You didn't hear him out, you never even asked how it went down, you just blamed him, and worse, you didn't blame me. You hit him where it hurt, you threw something on him, but you let me get away with it when it was equally my doing. You broke him, and you did it because you wanted him to hurt because of what he did to you..."

"Oh God," I rasp, putting my face in my hands.

"Don't make you a bad person, but you can't blame him for feelin' the way he does. You were his friend, above all else, and you never let him explain. You blamed him, you got on your parents side when they tried to take him down, and then you came back here and tried to ask for forgiveness."

When he puts it like that, I feel like a monster.

And that's what I am - a monster.

"God, what have I done?"

"Past, Tom Cat, you can't change it now..."

I meet Cade's eyes. "Thank you, for telling me."

"Ain't tellin' you nothin' you don't already know, deep down. I will also tell you I don't want you playin' around with Spike right now; he ain't good for you, Tom Cat. You had the right to know about the past, but now, you need to stay away."

"I need to fix what I broke," I protest.

"You can do that, but you need to keep your pants on when you do. Trust me, Tom Cat, I ain't doin' this to be an asshole, I'm doin' it 'coz he ain't no good for you."

"Isn't that my choice?" I whisper.

"Not if I'm fuckin' around," he growls and I sigh deeply. No point in trying to react right now, he won't hear of it. "Now, I'm goin' to head home and find my fiancé to punish her some more. We good?"

"We're always good," I smile weakly.

Cade returns my smile with full force. He steps forward, jerking me into his arms for a hug. I return it, wrapping my arms around his large frame.

"You know, for a biker, you're kinda sweet."

He grunts and pulls back. "You women, don't know what you're fuckin' talkin' about."

I giggle, and he flashes me another grin, before gripping his keys and walking to the door. When he gets to the opening, he turns and looks back at me.

"Don't chase him, Tom Cat. I mean it…let this one go, yeah?"

"Later, Cade," I say, ignoring his speech.

He nods at me, and steps out the door, and I find myself smiling. My heart hurts, my body aches for Spike, yet I'm smiling.

I'm smiling because there's a chance.

It might be tiny, but it's a chance.

And that's something - and something means I'll keep fighting for the friend I lost.

CHAPTER 3

PAST - CIARA

"Who's the motorcycle man?" Cheyenne asks me, flipping her long, blonde hair over her shoulder and peering out the window.

"That's Danny. He's a friend."

"A friend Mom and Dad won't like."

I shrug. "They won't know."

Chey turns and smiles, twisting her hair and securing it with a clip. "You into him?"

I snort. "No, he's just a friend."

She grins and her eyes twinkle with humor.

"Seriously, Chey, he's just a friend. Now, I have to go."

"All right, well you better be home before Mom gets here. You know she'll flip if you show up with Motorcycle Man down there."

I wave a hand, and grip my purse. "Yeah, I'll be home before her."

I turn and rush out the door, then down the stairs. I walk through our large home, until I reach the front door.

I step out, and instantly I smile. Danny is on his bike, grinning at me. He's beautiful in a way that just can't be described. His hair is long, sandy blonde and tied in a ponytail behind his head. He has these brown eyes that sometimes look black, they get so dark. I wave and hurry down the front stairs, surrounded by blooming red roses my mother planted months ago, grinning as I near him.

"Hey Tom Cat," he grins.

He's called me Tom Cat since the moment we met at a friend's party. As soon as he saw my oddly colored yellow eyes, he decided the name suited me.

"Hey Danny." I smile, getting on the back of his bike and taking the helmet he passes back to me.

"You ready? We're goin' to have a sweet day."

"What are we doing?" I ask, wrapping my arm around his waist.

"Secret, hang on."

He pulls the throttle and the bike lurches forward. We speed off down the street, and I breathe in deeply, getting a mix of the sea air and Danny's scent. God, he smells good. I might only be eighteen, but I know enough to know that Danny is the kind of man that has girls swooning. I wrap my arms tighter around him as we speed down the road.

I've been friends with Danny since I was seventeen, and since then we've spent most weekends together. He even picks me up for work in the mornings and drops me off in the afternoons.

We cruise down the highway, and I try to decide where it is Danny is taking me. When we pull up at a picnic ground with rolling hills and cute little picnic benches, and a massive swimming lake, my heart skips a beat. Danny doesn't show a great deal of affection. He can be hard when it comes to his feelings, but he shows them in other ways - ways like this. I slip off the back of the bike when Danny parks it, and lift my helmet off. My breath hitches as I admire the scenery; it's absolutely stunning. Danny gets off the bike and steps up beside me, and for a moment we're both quiet.

"Know how much you love swimmin'," he murmurs.

I turn to face him then I leap up and down, clapping my hands. He grins at me, flashing that deep, long dimple that completely transforms his face.

"Race you!"

He snorts, but I'm off and running before he even gets a chance to respond. I run up a hill, then down another until I can see the large lake, with it's perfectly clear water ahead. I'm just at the top of another hill when Danny catches up. He grips my waist and hurls me backwards. With a laugh, I latch onto him and take him with me when I fall.

We stumble down the large hill, bumping and grazing our skin as we roll. Yet the entire time, we're laughing. We hit the bottom with a thump, and Danny grips me, rolling us both until we flop into the water. I squeal as it surrounds me, freezing my skin and causing me to shudder. I manage to close my mouth and stop screaming just before we both go under. Danny doesn't let me go, he keeps his arms around me, and moments later we both re-surface.

"Fuck," he laughs, shaking his blonde hair around. "Didn't plan on entering quite so dramatically."

I giggle loudly. "You don't do anything in half measures, do you?"

"Hell no, Tom Cat."

I splash a heap of water at him, and he laughs, splashing some back. This starts a splashing war that has us both laughing so hard our stomachs hurt. By the time we get out of the water, we're soaked, laughing and completely content. We climb to the top of the hill and sit, staring out at the horizon. The lake meets more rolling hills, with a few scattered trees. I lean into Danny and like always, we chat freely. *Until the snake.* I'm sure one day I'll laugh about the snake, but for the moment, it's certainly not funny. It comes out of nowhere; suddenly it's just there, slithering toward us. I scream, leaping up. Danny is on his feet beside me in seconds.

"Stand still," he orders.

Like that's going to happen. Snakes are my biggest fear, and this one is huge. I scream so loudly that I hurt my own ears. My heart is beating heavily, and my entire body is tingly with fear.

So, I do the only thing that makes sense in that moment. I throw myself down the hill - headfirst. It wasn't my brightest moment, but in my panicked attempt to get away, I wasn't thinking. I roll and stumble, my body screaming at me to just stop. I can't, though. I roll and roll until I hit the flat ground just before the lake.

For a long moment I lay there, groaning in pain. My heart is still thumping, and my body aches everywhere.

Danny is down the hill in a second, and when I roll to look up at him, I expect to see worry in his expression - instead, he's smothering a laugh. As soon as our eyes meet, he throws his head back and roars with laughter. I cry out and cover my face, ashamed that I did something so stupid. Danny gets onto his knees, reaching for me but I slap his hands away.

"Aw, Tom Cat, come on," he laughs. "It was funny."

"It was not funny!" I cry, slapping his hands again.

"Tom Cat, it was fuckin' hilarious. Didn't you think of running the other way?"

"I was scared!" I protest, covering my face in shame.

"So you threw yourself down a hill?"

"Shut up, you asshole!"

"Aw, come here."

He grips me, pulling me onto his lap. His body is still shaking with laughter as he holds me tight.

"It's not funny, Danny."

"Kinda funny…"

"You're horrible."

"Can't help it. It's not every day a girl throws herself down a hill in front of you."

I can't help it. I burst out into a fit of giggles too. It was kind of stupid…

"You make my fuckin' days bright, Tom Cat."

I snuggle in closer, laughing along with him.

Danny makes me content.

Maybe one day, I'll tell him how much.

~*~*~*~

PRESENT - SPIKE

"Fuckin' find out," I bark down the phone, before slamming it closed.

I begin pacing the room. Fuck, things aren't going to plan. This is causing me to get far more involved than I would have originally liked. I won't stop, though. I won't stop until that cunt is on the ground, bleeding before me, begging to be saved. He's proving to be hard to find, though.

Fuck it. Fuck everything. My head isn't in the game like it should be, and it's starting to piss me off. Damn Ciara for coming in and confusing the fuck outta me.

"What's happenin' Prez?" Granger asks, lighting a smoke.

I reach for the packet, pulling one out and pressing it to my lips. I flick the lighter and inhale deeply. After a few puffs, I remove it and answer him.

"Hogan ain't in the location we thought he was. The fucker is not easy to find and it's startin' to piss me the fuck off!"

Granger nods, narrowing his eyes. "What now?"

"We're gonna fuckin' find him. We just gotta be smarter about it."

"What're you thinkin'?"

I meet his gaze. "We make a deal."

"Prez, that ended badly last time. You sure you wanna go back into that place?"

"Don't got nothin' to lose this time, so yeah, I wanna go back in. Only way to bring him out, is to get involved."

"It's a fuckin' risk."

I inhale the smoke again, feeling the nicotine swim through my veins. "It's a risk I'm willin' to take."

Granger nods, even though I can see he thinks my idea is fucked. I've thought of everything else; I've *tried* everything else. This is the only way to get vengeance, it's the only way to make him pay for what he did to Cheyenne. I have to make a deal. I have to get myself involved again. That means jumping back into the world of drugs.

"How'd you go with the girl?"

"What girl?" I mutter, snuffing out the cigarette.

"Ciara."

I flinch. Fuckin' Ciara. I haven't been able to get her out of my head all fuckin' night. The way she spoke, the emotion she showed. I had no fuckin' idea it went so deep. No fuckin' idea how much I'd hurt her. She has to know I'm not the man I was back then, she has to know wastin' her time with me is just that: wastin' time. I ain't worth the fight for anyone.

Besides, she fucked me over. I wasn't the only one who threw our friendship away. I can't let her in now; I got too much on the line. She's gotta stop this bullshit, and she's gotta stop it now.

"Fuck Ciara, she's messin' with my fuckin' head."

"What's she so desperate to get hold of you for?" he asks, taking another puff of his cigarette.

"Wants my forgiveness."

"For what?"

"For fuckin' me over instead of givin' me a chance after Chey died."

"Fuck man."

"Yeah," I grunt. "Fuck."

"Keep your distance yeah? You don't want her involved with what's goin' down.

"Think I didn't learn my fuckin' lesson last time?" I bark.

He puts his hands up. "I know you did Prez, I'm just doin' my job. She's got feelings there, anyone can see it. You need to knock it on the head. We can't have anyone gettin' involved. You need to find a way to get her to back off."

I don't answer him, I just grip my beer and turn, walking off. No fuckin' point in arguing with him. He thinks he's right.

Fucker probably is too.

I just don't know what I'm going to fuckin' do about it. The only thing I can think of doin', is going to speak to Jackson in an attempt to get her to stay away. It's not a bad idea - it's worth a fuckin' shot. I reach into my pocket and pull my cellphone out, and I flick through until I find his number. I can't go into Hell's Knights compound, so I'll have to meet him at the bar. He's the only option I've got now. This shit is far too dangerous for someone like Ciara to get involved in, and it's clear she's got a lot more to hash out with me.

"Yeah," Jackson answers.

"Jackson, it's Spike. Can we meet somewhere and talk?"

"What's up? Addison ain't shittin' you off again, is she?"

43

"Nah."

"Alright, where?"

"Bar in ten?"

"Be there."

"Cheers."

I flip the phone closed and head back into the sitting room. Granger looks up, lighting another smoke. Fucker smokes like a chimney.

"Goin' to meet Jackson."

He raises a brow. "What for?"

"To sort this Ciara shit out once and for all."

"Sure that's a good idea?"

I shrug, gripping my keys. "It's the only one I've got."

~*~*~*~*

The bar is quiet, but *she's* working. I curse as soon as I walk in and she notices me. Her yellow eyes widen. Fuck those eyes. They're the most beautiful fuckin' things I've ever seen. I never told her that. Probably never will. Her lips part slightly in shock, and she runs her long, delicate fingers through her thick, blonde hair. Fuck. I hate when she looks at me like that. Like I can be fixed. Like I'm a project. She can spit out how much she dislikes me as much as she wants - I see that damned look in her eyes every time she looks at me, so her words mean nothing. I know she wants to fix me. But she can't. I *won't* let her.

I turn my eyes away from her to see Jackson, sitting at the booth in the left corner. I walk over, shrugging off my jacket. It's just a sign of respect. He's not wearing his either. This is mutual ground, neither of us have a claim on it, so there's no need to show our patches.

He slides a beer across the table at me, and I wrap my heavily ringed fingers around it and take a sip. Jackson watches me, his eyes curious. He's looking at me like he's my fuckin' dad. I hate when he does that. Fuckin' Jack is too good for the life he lives. His heart is far too big.

"What's up, Spike?" he asks, lighting a cigarette.

"She's up."

I nod my head towards Ciara, who is now serving a dirty old man who is making no effort to try and hide his lingering eyes. That fucker. I want to go and drive a fist into his dirty fuckin' nose.

"Ciara?" Jackson asks, forcing my attention back to him.

"Yeah, Ciara."

"What's she doin'?"

I meet his gaze. "She's a problem for me."

Jackson narrows his eyes. "Why?"

"She's…I don't know how to put it, but she's tryin' to fix something here…between us…and it can't be fixed."

"I thought she got the message after the visit at the warehouse?"

"She didn't. Well, she did but she ain't willin' to give up. She's determined that we can get an old friendship back. It's a problem,

45

Jackson. I can't have her gettin' involved in my life, and the shit I'm doin'."

"What shit are you doin'?" he asks, giving me a hard stare.

I stiffen. "None of your business, Jack's. I don't ask what's goin' down between you and the Knights…same goes this end."

"It's my turf. Don't go bringin' motherfuckin' trouble here, Spike."

"Fuck, Jacks. I ain't gonna bring no trouble."

Jackson gives me a long, hard, glare, but then he sighs. "I don't own Ciara. I can't tell her what to do."

"She's under your protection, Jack's. Tell her to back down, that this ain't a clever thing she's doin'."

"She just wants your forgiveness. Maybe if you give it to her, she'll back off."

"No," I grunt. "She won't. It goes far deeper than forgiveness."

"Why don't you tell her to back down?"

"I have," I growl. "She won't have any of it. She won't back off. She thinks she can fix me. She's as stubborn as they come. That girl ain't backin' down anytime soon."

"Ignore her, eventually she'll go away."

I huff, clenching my fists, "You really don't know her, do you?"

Jack's growls. "Fine, Spike, I'll have a word with her. I'll try and get her to back off."

"Excuse me?"

I hear Ciara's angry voice and freeze. Well fuck, she wasn't supposed to hear. Slowly I turn, and I see her standing with two beers in her hands. She's glaring at me, and her eyes are alight with rage. Fuck.

"How. Dare. You."

"Ciara," Jackson begins, but she cuts him off with a glare.

"I thought better of you, Jackson. Is that all I am to you people? Some pathetic case you need to sort out?"

"It ain't like that…" he protests, but her eyes are back on mine.

Fuck those eyes.

"You," she snarls, leaning down so close her face is only inches from mine. She's panting with rage, and her words come out like fucking steel. "How dare you come in here and try to get Jackson to do your dirty work? You're pathetic, Spike. If you have something to say to me, man up and say it. You can try as hard as you fucking like, I'm not going to run away crying like the little girl I once was, because honey," she leans down, closer, "I got tough."

Then I feel the cold beer hit my chest. I jerk and my eyes widen as she tips the fuckin' beer down my front. The stare she's giving me is that of pure determination and, fuck, is that hunger? Fuck her. Fuck. Her. I growl and reach up, gripping her wrists.

"Quit what you're fuckin' doin' Ciara. *Now*."

A slow smirk stretches across her face and she stands up straight, smiling down at us as though we're just two customers she doesn't know.

"You two have a lovely night, and do call if you need more beers."

47

And just like that, she turns and walks off. I stare down at the beer that has now soaked my shirt and pants, and I curse loudly.

Well, fuck.

This ain't goin' to be easy.

The girl is gettin' under my skin.

CHAPTER 4

CIARA - PAST

"Where are you going, Ciara?" my mother asks, following me down to the front door.

She hasn't asked where I'm going, or whom I'm hanging out with for months. I know why she's doing it now, because Cheyenne had a problem with her friend and is now sulking in her room, and I'm expected to stay and give her some company. Not going to happen. Cheyenne certainly wouldn't do it for me. I meet my mother's gaze, and shrug my shoulders. It's so very teenager of me.

"I'm going out with a friend."

"Cheyenne is upset, it would be nice if you supported her like most sisters would."

I hate that. Just because she's my sister, doesn't mean I should have to drop everything for her. It takes much more to create a bond with someone, then just being blood related. Cheyenne has very rarely done anything for me. The whole 'family bond' thing doesn't really cut it in this household. Sadly, it never has, but my mother still expects me to want to drop everything to help Cheyenne out when she's in need. I don't mind helping her either, when her problems aren't petty and childish. I know for a fact this problem is just that.

"She'll be fine."

"Ciara, I am tired of all this attitude. You continually backchat me, and treat your sister like she's no more than an acquaintance. She's family. Family always comes first."

49

I snort. "Yeah, well, funny she doesn't have the same values when it comes to me."

"Cheyenne would die for you, don't be so selfish."

I roll my eyes, and she crosses her arms.

"Sorry, Mom, but I'm busy tonight. Perhaps you and Cheyenne can have a girls night, because you do enjoy those…"

I'm being sarcastic and mean, but I don't care.

She gives me the pained, hurt expression. "At least go and see her, she's hurting."

I sigh and growl loudly, before turning and storming up the stairs. I won't get to walk out of this house until I see Cheyenne and listen to her bitch about a friend who did wrong by her, even though she was likely the one who started it. I get to her room, swing the door open, and find her lying in bed, staring out the window. It's seriously like a movie. Next minute, it will be raining and a sad song will start playing. Can anyone say 'drama queen?'

"What happened?" I say, though my voice sounds snappy.

She rolls, pinning me with a glare. "You don't need to be here, Ciara. I know Mom is making you. I never asked you to care and we both know you don't."

Well shit, now she's making me feel bad. I drop my bag at the door and walk over, sitting on her bed.

"I wanted to make sure you were ok before I left."

Her eyes widen, and she sits. That's all it takes to get her to talk. "I'm not, it's Lisa."

Ah, the beloved best friend, with whom she fights on a daily basis. I nod my head, encouraging her to go on and trying to ignore the fact that Danny will be here in five minutes.

"So, I was seeing this guy…you remember him? Jerald?"

What a *stupid* name.

"Anyway, things were going really well until this afternoon when I saw him at the café with Lisa. They were laughing and joking, like they were on a date."

God save me.

"Maybe they just ran into each other…" I offer, trying to play it down as much as possible.

"Or maybe," she snaps, "she was trying to steal my boyfriend."

"Have you asked her?"

"No."

"So you could be moping over nothing? Unless you ask her, then you shouldn't be jumping to silly conclusions."

"I knew I shouldn't have spoken to you…" she growls. "You wouldn't understand men. You just hang out with that idiotic motorcycle man who you say you don't like, but we all know you do."

"You know nothing," I snap.

She hits me with that icy glare. "I know you want him. Better tell him soon, Ciara, or someone else will snap him up."

Every time. We cannot speak without her turning sour.

"Whatever," I say, turning and walking towards the door.

I don't bother saying anything else. Our heart to hearts always end in the same way – with Cheyenne and I fighting. We are always fighting, and the rare moments we aren't, go by so quickly I couldn't name any memorable ones. It's not that we don't love each other, because we do. It's just that we have nothing in common. She's outgoing, bubbly, and the light of most people's lives. I'm quieter, more reserved, and tend to stick in the shadows. It's how it's always been, and likely how it always will be.

I grip my bag, storm down the stairs and straight past my parents sitting in the living room. They don't even call out for me. Why would they? There's nothing for them to say to me. Not even a *be careful*. I rush down the front steps just as Danny pulls up. He sees the look on my face, and pulls off his helmet. I wave at him frantically, letting him know I don't want to stop. I just want to go. I need to get out of here, and away from the constant reminder that I'm second and I always will be. I lift the spare helmet off his bike, and climb on the back, saying nothing. He pulls his helmet back on, takes off, and we head to the movies.

I hold him tight the entire ride, struggling to steady out my emotions. When we pull up, and we're both off the bike, he turns to me. His big, brown eyes scan my face, and I can see he's worried about me, but he's also not the type to talk emotions. He's hard. It's just the way he is. His parents died at a young age, and he was left alone. He lived a hard life, and he's continued to live a hard life. He tried though, he went to school, got a job, and tried to build up something that had been so severely broken in the past. Sadly, it didn't last long. I know he's into some pretty bad stuff, even though he leaves me out of it.

"You okay, Tom Cat?"

"Just Cheyenne being an ass again," I say softly.

"Sorry," he says, it's the only thing he ever says, emotions aren't his strong point.

I wave my hand, plastering a smile on my face. "It doesn't matter. What are we watching?"

He grins, offering me his hand. I take it, and we walk into the theatre. Girls automatically turn and stare at Danny, it's hard not to. He's wearing dark denim jeans, a tight black shirt, and heavy black boots. He's got a few colorful tattoos running up his left arm, and he's wearing a great deal of silver jewelry. He looks like a bad ass, and let's face it, girls love a bad boy.

"You wanna go funny, or scary?" he asks, as we scour the titles, still hand in hand.

"Scary."

He smirks, and we order two tickets to some horror flick that I have no doubt we will laugh the entire way through. It's our thing. We come to the movies, and we laugh. It doesn't matter if it's a scary, funny, sad, or downright boring movie. We laugh, and we have a great time. We're both the kind of people who will laugh right at the moment everyone else is crying. I remember watching the Titanic when it came back on big screen for the second time. Right at the end, people were blubbering and a complete mess, but Danny and I? Nope. I'll never forget Danny's comment right at the end, when Rose has just let Jack go, and she whispers, "I'll never let go, Jack." Danny snorted, and stared at the screen in horror as Jack sunk. His words? "She just fuckin' let him go!"

We laughed for days about it.

That's just us.

And our friendship might not be for everyone, but it's ours, and because it's ours, I love it.

CHAPTER 5

CIARA - PRESENT

"I'm so sorry," I say when my boss comes back from his few nights away to see the mass amounts of chairs and tables missing because of the brawl that broke out in the bar the other night. I've managed to clean most of it up during my last few shifts, but there were some things I couldn't replace.

He's glaring at me, panting angrily. "You fucked half of my fuckin' bar!"

"I'm sorry, it was a bad call on my part. I'll do whatever it takes to make it up to you."

"Damn right you will. You're goin' to go a week without pay to replace what you fuckin' broke."

I want to argue, but there's no point. I'll only lose my job, and I need this job. It's all I have. If I lose it, I have to go home, and there ain't no way in hell I'm going to crawl back to my parents. *No way in hell.*

"Of course," I say, my voice small.

"You're lucky you've still got a job. If I could find girls easier, I would have fired your ass."

"Thank you for giving me a chance."

I turn and walk away before he can answer. I feel awful for what I've done. This bar is the only one in town the locals can come to and enjoy themselves, and I had half of it smashed to pieces because of my terrible behavior. That's on me.

I head into the backroom, and the girl that's on with me, Jenny, is just changing. She smiles at me, a wicked little gleam in her eye. I can't help but return the smile. Jenny is a devil at heart; she would have gotten a complete kick out of what went down the other night.

"I heard you caused a bar fight while I was away."

"Yeah, I did that."

"With hot bikers…" She grins, wiggling her brows.

I raise my brows at her. "How did hot bikers become involved in this?"

"You tell me." She winks.

I grin at her then open my locker to pull out my skirt and tiny blue top that is compulsory for us 'bar bitches'. I slip my top off, and shimmy into the tiny blue tank. I quickly tie my hair up and throw on some basic make-up, then I turn and answer Jenny's question.

"It wasn't hot bikers, it was Spike and his boys…"

"Oh god, Spike was the one fighting? My panties just got wet."

Mine did at the time too, but she doesn't need to know that.

"He was mega pissed."

"Totally the best way for a man like him to be. So, what happened?"

I shrug. "He came in, defended me and took me home."

"Spike took you home? I thought you two hated each other?"

"We don't hate each other…as such."

"He came to your defense? What have I missed here?"

I grin at her, and lean down to slip on my shoes. "Nothing. I swear."

"What punishment did Joe give you?"

"A week without pay."

"Ouch," she says crinkling her pretty nose.

Jenny is an attractive girl, the kind of girl that gets most men's attention. She's Latin, and has these dark brown eyes, perfect olive skin and straight, thick black hair. She has a slight accent, which just makes them want her a whole lot more.

"Yeah, ouch. I guess I'm eating crackers all week."

She frowns at me. "Is it that bad?"

"It's not easy paying my own rent, food and college fees."

"Sorry. I wish I was here so I could have stopped it all before it happened."

I laugh, and wave my hand. "It's fine, it was my own stupid fault."

She chuckles. "Yeah, well, let's get to it."

We spend the first two hours of our shift bringing out some old chairs from the storage room and making it look a little more respectable for Joe. When the doors open, I get behind the counter and start serving as soon as the first group comes in. We have a hen's night on, so one side of the bar is covered in pink streamers, balloons and pretty table decorations. I can't help but smile when the group of girls comes in, dressed in pink fairy outfits. They are all carrying little wands, and giggling the way all girls should when out enjoying the upcoming marriage of a friend, or family member.

I feel my chest tighten. I'll never have that kind of feeling. My sister is dead. I have no one left, because my parents continue to somehow blame me. I guess I was the one that originally brought Spike home, so that must mean I am to blame. I turn my attention back to the glass I'm drying, and focus on steadying my breathing. No point in getting upset over something that can't be changed.

I turn, throwing the glasses in the dishwasher, and then I get back to serving. That's when he walks in. I hate that he's decided to come in tonight, because it's just a shitty night for me. After I tipped beer all over him the last time he was here, I honestly didn't think he'd show his face again.

Spike and his club members take a seat at one of the round, corner tables. I peer over at them, and Spike looks up at the same moment. Our eyes meet, but I quickly turn mine away. I watch as Joe walks over, gives them a stern lecture, and then, as if nothing ever happened, he's laughing with them.

I feel Jenny slide up beside me as I'm watching them, and I know she's going to say something. She's getting a great deal of satisfaction over the fact that Spike being here is making me completely uncomfortable.

"You're on his table tonight."

Of course I am. I turn and give her a look. She puts her hands up innocently.

"Hey, I got given the hens, be grateful."

"You're awful Jenny," I mutter.

"Oh come on, look at him."

We both turn to stare. He's wearing a bandana tonight, and bits of his messy blonde hair and stick out from beneath it. His shirt matches the dark blue bandana, and his black jeans are perfectly fitting for his body. His leather jacket is sitting on the table beside him, and his heavy black boots are crossed under the table. The colorful tattoos on his arms are showing, along with the thick bracelets around his wrists. God damn, he can pull off the biker look so incredibly well. I turn, and switch my gaze back to Jenny.

"I've looked…"

"Well." She wiggles her brows. "Enjoy yourself."

Sighing, I turn and walk around the bar and over to Spike's table. He looks up at me when I stop, and his eyes slide over the outfit I'm wearing. Yes, I know, it's revealing. My black skirt is short, and when I say short…I mean short. My top sits above my belly button, so basically, most of my body is on view for perverts to gawk at. It's Job of the Year, I tell you.

"Nice outfit," he grumbles.

"What can I get you boys?" I ask, ignoring him.

"You can come over here and sit on my lap." One of the bikers grins.

Spike shoots him a glare. "Fuckin' pipe down, Muff."

The man named Muff, grins. "Just givin' her a chance to take a break."

"As much as I'd love to, I can't take a break." I smile sweetly. "Now, drinks?"

Spike is watching me, I can feel his gaze, and it's causing little shivers to run through my body. God, I hate that he constantly has my body coming to life. Fucker.

"You seein' anyone, sweet thing?" Muff asks.

I smile at him; it's kind of hard not to. He's sweet…in a creepy, cute kind of way. He grins back at me. He's not a bad looking man. He wouldn't be a great deal younger than Spike, and it's possible he's even the same age. I'm fairly sure Spike is around twenty-nine.

Muff has a youthful face, and long red hair. He kind of reminds me of one of those Scottish men.

"Not right now." I grin.

"Well, keep me in mind yeah?"

"She ain't keepin' you anywhere, now shut the fuck up," Spike growls at him.

Muff puts up his hands. "Whoa, Prez, just playin'."

"Get us some beers," Spike growls, giving me a hard look.

I glare at him. "Where are your manners, Danny?"

The boys burst out laughing, and Spike's eyes flare angrily.

"I'll show you fuckin' manners in a minute. Don't fuck with me, Ciara. Get us some beers."

I cross my arms and stare at him, refusing to move until he asks nicely. He crosses his arms and glares right back.

Fine, two can play at this game. I turn, walk to the bar and get some beers, then I return…minus one. I give all the guys a beer, except Spike. I smile sweetly at him, and just as I'm about to turn away I say, "Didn't anyone ever teach you that manners get you everywhere?"

I grin the entire way back to the bar, and even more when Spike has to walk up and get served by Jenny, who, mind you, thinks all her Christmas' have come at once. My grin widens as I watch him stomp back to the table. Completely satisfied with myself, I turn and continue serving.

I know by the amount of people piling in, that the night is going to be a big one. The hens are already chatting up random men that walk in. A few of them have sauntered over to Spike's table and fluttered their eyelids. I catch a glimpse of Spike laughing, and pulling one of them onto his lap. He gives me a smirk when I see his eyes on me. Oh Spike, you're playing with fire.

"Another round for Spike's table," Jenny says ten minutes later, sliding me a tray.

I pick it up, and walk over. Spike's hands are up Blondie's skirt. Screw him for being such a jerk. He's rubbing me up the right way, and clearly…her the right way, too. She's clutching him, running her lips over Spike's neck. Our eyes meet for the briefest moment, and I hope he sees nothing in my gaze.

I grin, putting the beer down and peering around the room. Joe is out back; five minutes won't matter. I lean over the table, knowing my breasts are popping out enough in my top to send most men over the edge. Muff's, eyes widen. I grin at him.

"See something you like?"

He grins, flashing me two cute dimples. "You know I do, princess."

I grin back. "I could use that break now. You want to join me outside?"

Nodding, Muff stands and slides out of the booth. Spike is glaring at me, I can feel his eyes burning holes into the side of my head, but I don't once look. I take Muff's hand and yell out to Jenny that I'm going on break, then I head outside with him.

We take a seat at the smokers' table, and he lights one up, offering me one. I'm not a big smoker, but every now and then I don't mind enjoying one. I take the smoke, and lean forward and let him light it for me. I notice the tattoos running up his arms: they're quite colorful and extensive. I take hold of his wrist and inspect them.

"You've got some great work here."

"Yeah, took a long time to get those tatts how I wanted them."

"I like them."

"Yeah?"

I release his arm and grin up at him. "Yeah. So, tell me, what's your real name?"

He gives me a lazy half-smile. He really is an attractive man. It surprises me to see him alone. "Brian."

I smile. "Brian…how did you get Muff?"

He laughs hoarsely. "You know what a muff is, princess?"

I giggle. It's unexpected and a little girly. "Yeah, I do."

"Well, that's how I got my nickname…I got a thing for…well…muff."

I snort and roll my eyes, taking a deep pull of the cigarette. "Don't all men?"

He laughs again, and leans back against the wall. "Yeah, but not the way I like 'em. I could spend hours with my face buried in a muff, hours and hours. I couldn't care less if the girl didn't touch me once, so long as I got to taste her over and over again."

My cheeks flush. Wow, he really does like women's...bits.

"Well, I guess you do take it to the next level. Your girlfriends must like you a whole lot."

His deep, rumbling laugh warms me somehow. "Yeah, princess, they sure fuckin' do."

I hear the door open, and turn my head to see Spike walking out, Blondie attached to his side. A swell of pure pleasure fills my chest. I know the look on Spike's face. He came out here to check on me— even though he didn't ditch Blondie, he's still checking. That warms something inside me, and it fills me with even more determination.

"You better not be harrassin' girls, Muff," Spike says, lighting up a smoke.

Blondie giggles and leans over, taking a drag. Spike grins down at her, and then lowers his head and captures her lips in his.

My heart hammers against my chest. I know what he's doing. He's making a point of trying to piss me off. He's trying to make me mad at him so I'll walk away. Oh Spike, you really don't know the girl I am anymore. Old me would have ran off crying, new me...she can play. I turn to Muff, and continue our conversation as though Spike didn't walk out.

"So tell me, Muff, is there a lucky girl getting all that special attention from your right now?"

He crushes his smoke out. "Nope, no lucky girl right now. My tongue is havin' a break."

"What a shame," I say, my voice far more husky than I'd like. "I could use a decent tongue."

Spike makes a choking sound, and Blondie giggles.

"I think we interrupted something here…" she says.

I'm grinning on the inside. Believe me.

"I'll keep that in mind," Muff says, grinning at me.

I'm almost sure he knows what I'm doing, and I'm grateful to him for playing along. He has a sparkle in his eyes, like he's enjoying it as much as I am.

"You just call me, and I'll be there."

"I don't have your number," I say, grinning at him.

"Come here princess."

I lean over, and he reaches into his jacket pocket and pulls out a pen. He leans down, taking hold of my side, then he begins to write his number on the top curve of my breast. I flush, but I'm so completely grateful to him right now because when I lift my eyes, the glare Spike's giving me could cut glass. When Muff is done, he leans back and gives me a subtle wink.

"Don't you have a fuckin' job to do?" Spike growls.

I lean over, gripping Muff's face and bringing his lips to mine. I only peck him, but it's enough. I pull back and Muff is still grinning. "Thanks for the break."

"Anytime princess," he says nodding at me as I hop off the seat and saunter past Spike.

When I get inside, I'm cheering. That's two for Ciara and zero for Spike.

~*~*~*~*

The night is long, and people fill the bar quickly. The hens begin squealing, singing karaoke and causing an uproar with the men as they saunter around, looking for a good time. My night is so busy, I don't get much of a chance to pay attention to anything else going on around me. We really do need more girls working on a night like this. My feet ache, and my hands are sore from opening so many beers. I could use the opener, but it's so much quicker just to flip them off with my fingers.

"Hey babe," Jenny says between pouring drinks. "Can you run out back and grab more whiskey, we're out."

"Sure," I say, spinning on my sore feet and heading out back.

I head down the halls to the back room, and I slip inside, flicking on the light. I don't see them right away, because of how they're positioned. Two bodies, pressed against a rack of wine. The first glimpse I get, I only see a woman, all legs, arms, and hair. Then I see the man in her grips, and I recognize him right away. It's Spike, and he's fucking Blondie in our storage room. My heart leaps into my throat, as I let my eyes adjust and travel over them.

65

Blondie has her back against the rack of wine; her long hair is loose and flowing down over Spike's back. Her legs are around his waist, her arms around his neck, and her head is buried in his shoulder. He's fully clothed, except for the fact that his jeans are slightly lowered. He's thrusting hard, fast, and deep. I can hear the friction as his jeans hit her skin. Blondie lifts her head from Spike's shoulder, and her eyes meet mine. I can't seem to move my legs, I want to, but I can't. She opens her mouth and makes a small squeaky sound. Spike turns his face, and his eyes connect with mine.

He tilts his head to the side, and slides his fingers up, cupping her breast. He knows what he's doing to me, he knows exactly how this will feel, and he's rubbing it in. Part of me, a small part, wonders if he knew I'd come in here. He's so determined to make me hate him, and he's doing a fine job at it. He continues to thrust his hips, and Blondie seems to forget I'm there. She drops her head back, and thrusts her breast into his hand. He begins fucking her harder, and I can see the pleasure in his eyes as he watches me. I am so incredibly angry at how cold he's behaving right now, but there's no way in hell he's seeing that.

I want to give him an angry reaction. I'd love nothing more than to lift a bottle of wine, and thrust it at his head, but that's what he wants. He's so sure hurting me is the way to get rid of me, so sure I'll run away crying and hate him forever. God he's wrong, all he's doing is making me that much more determined. I'm wild with rage, how dare he bring a girl in here to try and piss me off. How fucking *dare* he! He won't get the desired reaction from me though, hell no, he's going to get a dose of his own medicine. I let a slow, sexy smirk creep across my lips, and I see his eyes widen in a moment of confusion. Yeah, that's right baby, that isn't the reaction you wanted is it. Let's see how this goes down.

I lift my hand, letting him get a clear vision of it, then I splay my fingers, and I place it over my breast. Spike's eyes widen, but I continue, making out that his reaction doesn't affect me at all. I slide my fingers down my chest and over my belly, and then I slip them up my shirt. I find my own hardened nipple, and I pinch it. A whimper escapes my throat, and Spike begins thrusting harder. It's affecting him, and that's exactly what I want. I know how kinky Spike is, and I know how much he likes that bit of extra something to get him over the edge.

I move my other hand, sliding it up my thigh, and under my skirt. Spike growls loudly, and makes the girl in his grips scream as he tightens his grip on her breast. I'm aroused, I feel it the moment my fingers graze my panties. I spread my legs a little, and run my fingers up and down, before slipping them inside and finding my slick heat. I know Spike has a glimpse of my exposed flesh, not enough for a full view, but enough to let his imagination run wild.

I tilt my head back, exposing my long, lean neck, and I moan loudly as I begin to stroke my aching clit. Spike makes a hissing sound, and the slapping of his skin against Blondie gets louder and louder as he picks up his pace. I lift my head up, and meet his gaze. I can see he's close, it's written all over him. His face is tight, the veins in his neck are bulging, and his thrusting is becoming urgent. I know how much Spike likes to watch, and that's why he's so aroused. If I stop right now, he'll struggle to find his pleasure.

And that's exactly why I stop right as he's about to come. His eyes widen, and he makes a pained wincing sound as I remove my fingers from my throbbing flesh, pop them into my mouth, and lick my arousal off. Then I spin, gripping a bottle, and flashing him a grin. I walk out of the room to the sounds of his loud, angry, cursing. Spike might think hurting me is the best way to push me out of his life, but what he didn't add into his little plan, is that I've thought of every possible thing he can do, and I've made sure I have something to throw back at him. I say bring it, biker. I decided I'm going to fight, and when I fight, I don't back down.

That's three for Ciara, and none for Spike.

~*~*~*~*

PRESENT - CIARA

Having no money sucks. It really sucks. Five days in, and I'm living on the cheapest food, and my car is just about out of gas. In fact, it's so close that I'm fairly sure I'll only just make it home after my shift tonight, which I might add, is a crappy one. Jenny is moody, Joe is away and the bar is packed. I've been here for eight hours, and I'm far, far over it. My shift finished an hour ago, but the girl who was meant to take over is late. Seriously, how do some people hold jobs? I couldn't afford to be late. Truly, an hour's worth of pay can mean extra food, an extra few miles in my car - hell, maybe a treat once in a while.

"She's here," Jenny grumbles into my ear.

I turn and see Susie coming through the door. She's hungover, I can see it a mile away. Too bad for her. I've been here all day and I need to go home, shower, and snuggle up with my cat and watch a tragic movie. I'm in one of those moods.

"Thank god," I sigh, turning on my aching feet and heading out back.

I dress quickly, pulling on a pair of old shorts and a tank. I grip my purse, my keys and phone, then I spin on my heel and head back out. I wave to Jenny and Susie, but they don't notice because Susie is getting her head chewed off by Jenny. Good; the girl needs to learn some better work ethics. I slip past the customers and out the front door. I find my car, slide in and start it up. The cooling kicks in right away, and I sit for a moment, just letting it wash over me. While I do this, I stare down at the little arrow that shows me how

69

much gas is left. It's gone below empty but my car is pretty good on gas, so I'm almost sure it will make it home without a problem.

I get driving, and am halfway home when the car begins to splutter. That's fucking Murphy's Law! My eyes widen and I curse loudly as it begins to slow down. You've got to be fucking kidding me? This is *NOT* happening right now. As she comes to a complete stop, I manage to just get her off the road. I get out, letting off a frustrated bellow. I kick the tire so hard I hurt my toe, badly. Hobbling, I grip my hair and yell loudly to the sky. God dammit. I'm ten miles from home, it's dark, late and the chances of anyone coming past in the next few hours is slim at this time of the night. Dammit, fuck my stupid mistakes. If I didn't trash the bar, I would have been paid and my car would have enough damn gas! Fuck.

I get back in, turning the key. She splutters, but doesn't start. Tears well in my eyes, and my chest begins to ache. Why is this happening to me? God dammit. I had a good fucking life. I get out of the car again, kicking the door closed. I hobble into the trees angrily, hot tears running down my cheeks. There's little to no cell phone service here, so I have to walk to try to get some. My toe is throbbing, and my heart hurts. When did my life go so wrong? I had it all worked out. I was dating, I was getting ready to go to school, I was finding my happiness…and then Chey died and everything spiraled out of control. I tilt my head up to the sky, and I scream.

"Why did you go and fucking die, Chey? Why? You left so much destruction behind. You left people broken. They blame me, you know? It's my fault! I was the one who brought Spike home! They don't smile anymore, *he* doesn't smile anymore. Why did you have to go and fuck everything up? You always were so selfish! Everything had to go your way! I had a life, I was going to college, I was going to meet a nice man and be happy but then you went and died. Now everything is fucked up, everything is broken and here I am, on the side of the road, because I can't afford gas. Damn you, Cheyenne, *DAMN YOU!*"

I'm screaming so loudly I miss the sound of the Harley-Davidson. When I lower my head, I see him. The light from his bike illuminates him, and he just stands there, arms crossed, watching me scream at nothing. Of course he'd be the fucking one to stop. Of course! Tears blur my vision, but I can see the pain in his face, even through them. My heart hammers, and I hate that he's seen me like this - vulnerable, angry and alone. He continues to see the weak parts of me. My breathing is heavy, my chest rises and falls dramatically. It takes me a moment to calm myself enough to speak, and when I do it comes out as a broken rasp.

"Fuck off, Spike. I don't need you here."

"What the fuck are you doin' out here, alone, at this time of the night?" he says, his voice raspy, too.

"My car ran out of gas!" I scream at him. "Because you and your friends trashed the bar and I had to pay for it. I can't even afford to put fucking gas in my car!"

I laugh now, but it's not a happy, cheerful laugh. It's a broken, "go figure" laugh. Spike's eyes scan my body, as if checking for injury. His eyes settle on the leg I'm lifting just slightly off the ground because it hurts so badly.

"You're hurt."

"I kicked my car, it's fine."

"Get on the bike, and I'll take you home."

"Fuck you!" I hiss.

He crosses his arms. "Swear at me as much as you like, I ain't leavin' you here alone."

"Why do you keep coming to my rescue, Spike? You don't even like me. Stop wasting my time, and yours. Just leave me alone."

"I wasn't comin' to your rescue, I was ridin' past and saw a car with the doors open and no one in it. Didn't know it was yours till I heard you screamin'."

"Whatever. I'm going to call Cade, or Addison…I don't need your help."

"Cade and Addi are out of town."

"Well I'll call Jackson!"

"What for? I'm already here?"

I throw my hands up and snarl, "Because I don't want you here! Because I don't want to go anywhere near you. Because I fucking hate you, Danny!"

He jerks, and his eyes widen, as though I have slapped him across the face. He's shocked. Well good, I don't care anymore. I'm sick of fucking caring for someone who just refuses to see it. He's so determined to push me away.

"This is all your fault!" I continue, my voice sounding choked up. "It's all your fault! Yours and hers. You two were so selfish, you never thought of anyone else. I have no home, no family, because they don't want me in their lives because I'm not good enough! Because I'm not Cheyenne!"

"I'm not the only fuckin' selfish one. You are too, Ciara. You fucked off, you never even gave me a motherfuckin' chance. We were friends, and you fucked me over as much as I fucked you over."

"We were never friends!" I bellow. "I was just a way to get to Cheyenne. You fucked me, to get to Cheyenne."

"That's fuckin' bullshit!" he roars. "It's fuckin' bullshit! I cared about you long before she came into the picture. What do you call all those times we spent together? I didn't fuckin' know her then. We were friends before her, and it didn't fuckin' matter to you when you stood in that courtroom and told the judge I was a piece of shit!"

"You are!" I scream, shaking. "You are such an asshole Spike. You saw her, and suddenly I didn't matter. We were friends, you're right, but that didn't matter to you when you fucked me to get back at her!"

"That's not the only motherfuckin' reason I did it!" he snarls, clenching his fists.

"Really, well why did you do it then? Did you feel like popping a fucking cherry?"

"I did it 'cause I fuckin' wanted to. I didn't fuckin' know you were a fuckin' virgin! God dammit, Ciara. You think you know every fuckin' thing!"

"You're such a liar! You lie so much you forget what it is you started lying about. Don't you dare try and tell me you didn't know I was a virgin. You knew I wasn't seeing anyone, we were friends for years. You *KNEW!"*

"I didn't fuckin' know!"

I storm towards him, only to realize my foot is still throbbing. I trip as soon as my weight falls on it and I stumble, going ass over

73

head into the dirt, hurting my toe further. That does it for me. I scream angrily and pummel my fists into the dirt. I am so sick of this hurt, so sick of feeling like everything is because of me, everything is my fault, everything that went wrong, is on me.

"I was never enough for you," I rasp. "I cared about you. Fuck Spike, I loved you. But you didn't fucking see me. You just saw her. I was never pretty enough, never good enough, I couldn't compare. You didn't even kiss me! Do you know that? You fucked me, you put your tongue in my pussy, your mouth on my breasts but you didn't fucking kiss me. Not once. That's how much respect you showed me that night! *NONE*!"

He takes an angry step forward and reaches down, gripping my shoulders and hurling me up so I'm flat against him. The emotion between us right now is huge, it's consuming me, making my heart hurt, making my head ache. I hate that I want him so much. I love that I have him right now. I fucking love and hate everything that's happening.

"That what this is fuckin' about? That I never fuckin' kissed you?"

"It's about so much more, but you can't fix what you did now. It's done."

"Can't fix that, can fix this."

He leans down, and his lips are on mine before I can protest. My mouth opens as a strangled gasp leaves it. I flinch, and a flood of warmth travels through my veins, making my entire body feel like it's on fire. I shudder as he presses his mouth harder against mine. His lips are soft and full, his body large and firm as he presses himself against me. My hands are limp beside me. I can't move, I'm like a rag doll in his arms. His tongue finds mine and fireworks explode in my head; I'm almost sure I see stars. Then suddenly, my hands come to life, and I thrust them into his hair, tugging him closer. My mouth is devouring his, my tongue dancing with his in hungry, angry strokes. He growls and presses a hand to my lower back, pressing my body up against his hard erection. I untangle one of my hands from his hair, and run it down his firm back. I slip it under his shirt and feel his hot, hard skin. It's taut, and his muscles bunch as I slide my fingers up, feeling every inch of his muscled flesh.

Then his mouth is off mine, and I'm stumbling backwards. He's reeling backwards just as quickly, his eyes confused. He's panting so heavily I can see his chest is rapidly rising and falling. His eyes are wild, like he's just made a huge mistake.

I press my fingers to my swollen lips. Did that just happen? Did Spike just…kiss me? I've never been kissed like that in my entire life, not once. That kiss, it was a kiss of passion. It was real, beautiful, gut wrenching, soul shattering…but mostly, it was mind fucking. What did it mean? Spike's fists are clenched, and his eyes are a mix of anger and lust.

"Now we're even. Get on the bike," he rasps.

He just kissed me to make it even? My heart falls. Everything in my world stops as pain washes through my chest.

"I don't want to go with you," I whisper.

"Get on the fuckin' bike, so help me god, I'll fuckin' put my hand to your ass, Ciara."

His voice is like ice. Swallowing, I struggle to step forward, but all I manage is a wince of pain. Growling, Spike steps closer and I expect him to hurl me forward and hurt me even further, but instead he scoops me into his arms…gently. He carries me up to his bike and puts me on the back.

I stare down at my clothes: I'm covered in dirt. Spike thrusts a helmet at me, and, with shaky hands, I put it on. He walks over to my car, closing and locking it, before climbing onto the bike in front of me. I wrap my arms around him, not wanting anymore arguing, and we speed off into the night, both of us no doubt as confused as the other.

We pull up out front of my house, and I quickly climb off the bike. I'm limping quite heavily right now, but all I can think about is the pain in my heart.

I'm surprised when Spike gets off the bike too. He has no reason to be here with me, and I don't understand why he feels the need to continue to pretend like he does. He doesn't want to be here, I know that as well as he does. I don't want his pity just because my sister would want him taking care of me. I'm no-one's charity case, especially not someone that is being forced to look out for me because of guilt.

"You need to let me look at that foot."

I stop hobbling towards my door and turn, staring at him.

"Why?"

He crosses his arms, and throws his leg over the bike before striding towards me. "'Cause it's my fault you ran outta gas in the first place, so I'm goin' to make sure you're okay before I leave. Don't bother fuckin' arguin' with me, Ciara. It won't change my mind."

I open my mouth to argue, but quickly close it again. The look on his face is that of threat. He's not going to back down. With a deep, defeated sigh, I turn and continue hobbling towards the door.

I unlock it and step inside. Spike follows close behind me. I head into the kitchen, desperate for a hot drink and some painkillers. I hear Spike stop walking, and turn to see him staring at a picture of Cheyenne and I after they were married. I think it was one of their anniversary parties. It was, without a doubt, the hardest day of my life. Seeing the man who stole my heart, celebrating his love with another woman is something I could never live through again. But I did it, for her.

"Remember that day…" he says, his voice gruff.

"Yeah," I say in a small, weak voice. "Me too."

Our eyes meet for a moment, before I quickly turn back to the boiling water.

"You need to sit so I can look at your foot."

"I'm fine, it's…"

"Sit the fuck down," he barks.

I turn, giving him a glare. He crosses his arms, narrowing his eyes and challenging me, just daring me to argue.

"I need to shower and…"

"Sit. Now."

Growling, I hobble over to the lounge and sit down. Spike kneels in front of me and grips my foot, slipping off my shoe. He raises it and inspects it. I can see it's swollen and purple. Great. Just what I need right now. Something else to stop me from working.

"Lookin' like it could be fracture, or at the least, badly bruised. You need to keep this up for a few days."

"You can't be serious," I cry. "I have a job I need to go to!"

"Well, you ain't goin' to it."

I start to cry. It's pathetic, but I can't help it. Big fat tears stream down my cheeks. Dammit. Why does this keep happening?

"Ah shit," Spike grunts. "Don't start cryin'."

"Can you just leave?" I snap through my tears. "Just go and leave me the hell alone."

"Hey," he growls. "Look at me."

I keep my eyes directed at my lap.

"Now, Tom Cat."

Hearing him call me Tom Cat has shudders wracking my body. It's been so long, and the swell of emotion in my chest is nearly too much, but I lift my face, meeting his gaze.

"I might not be a great person, but I'm not enough of a fuckin' prick to leave a girl who is hurt because of me. I also won't let her take the fucked up end of the stick because of my actions. You tell me how much you need to cover you for a few days off, and I'll give it to you."

"I'm not going to do that, Spike."

"You don't get a choice. Give me a number, or I'll make one up."

"No."

78

"Fine," he says, pulling his wallet from his back pocket. He grips a wad of cash out and thrusts it at me. "That should cover it."

I stare at the cash in my hands, and gape. "I wouldn't make this much in a week."

"Fuckin' need to speak with Joe about how much he pays his girls," he says under his breath, and then he meets my eyes again. "I fucked that bar, 'cause I took the first swing. It ain't on you and you shouldn't have to miss out 'cause of me. Take it, don't argue, and we'll both go our separate ways."

"Are we ever going to be friends again, Spike?"

He narrows his eyes, and his expression becomes hard. "Don't mistake this kindness for us being friends. I'm doing it because I fucked up. There ain't nothin' more to it. You ain't ever gonna be more than an acquaintance, Ciara."

Ouch. That burns. It burns me right down to my core. His words affect me in a way I wasn't prepared for, and I do the only thing I can to cover the hurt. I get angry.

"Get out, Spike," I hiss. "I don't need your fucking pity. I've lived this long without your 'kindness', and I don't need it now. If you can't even be my friend, then do me a favor, and get the fuck out of my life. I should have never trusted you, and I should have never wasted so many years of my life wanting something that was clearly never worth fighting for. I'm done, Spike. I'm done trying to fix you. You're right, there's nothing good left in you. Nothing at all."

I get to my feet and I thrust the cash at him. Then I turn and walk off down towards the hall. Just as I reach it, I turn and growl, "You know where the door is."

Then I disappear into the darkness. I stand there for long moments, just listening. I hear him go - the door slams, his bike starts up, and he speeds off down the street.

My chest hurts. It aches so much that I struggle to get a steady breath. I hobble back into the lounge and my eyes fall on the coffee table. And I stop breathing. My vision blurs as tears well in my eyes. A strangled gasp escapes my throat and I grip my chest, as if that will take the pain away. There on the table is the cash, but that's not what tears my heart to pieces. It's the bracelet sitting on top of it. A bracelet made of leather, with silver beads representing friendship.

A bracelet I gave Spike a long time ago.

A bracelet that promised lifelong friendship.

A bracelet that swore my loyalty to him.

A loyalty I just broke.

God, what am I fucking doing?

CHAPTER 6

PAST - SPIKE

"Come on Tom Cat, you're takin' your sweet time!" I yell out from the bottom of Ciara's stairs.

We're meant to be headed out to the fair, but bloody Ciara is takin' her sweet fuckin' time getting ready. As always. I lean against the railing and I run my fingers through my thick, blonde hair. I really need to get rid of this, it's startin' to piss me off. I just don't have it in me to look after hair this long.

I peer up the stairs again. Fuck, women can take their sweet ass time when they want to.

"I'm coming!" she yells.

I grin. I can't help it. Ciara has that thing about her, she's like sunshine and rain, all mixed in one sweet ass package.

"So, you're the Motorcycle Man she's been babbling about."

I hear the sweet, silky voice behind me, and turn, letting my eyes fall on a very attractive girl that has to be Ciara's sister, Cheyenne. She's told me a lot about her, but I've not had the chance to meet her. Grinning, I take her in. She's different to Ciara, she's missing those wild cat eyes, but she's equally as beautiful. She leans her hip against a nearby cabinet, and lets her eyes travel down my body. Is this girl seriously checking me out right now?

"And you must be the Sister."

She gives me a devilish smile, and steps forward, extending her hand. "Cheyenne, and you are?"

"Spike."

She raises her brows. "Spike? I thought your name was Danny?"

"I'm Danny to Ciara, but to everyone else, I'm Spike."

"I didn't know you were so…hot," she says, letting those eyes travel over me again.

I laugh huskily. "Yeah, well, good genes."

"I'll say," she giggles. "So, tell me what your intentions are with my Sister?"

I snort. "Ain't no intentions there, darlin'. She's my best friend."

"Ah, so it's not a romance?"

"No."

I fuckin' wish it were sometimes.

"And why is that, Spike?" she purrs, sliding her tongue out and running it over her bottom lip.

Fuck. Ciara's sister is flirting with me. Openly. Not holding anything back.

"Wouldn't you like to know?"

She steps forward, running a finger down the front of my shirt. Fuck. Fuck. *Fuck.* If only Ciara was this outgoing, maybe then we wouldn't be dancing around feelings that we both know are there, yet neither of us want to admit. It's the fear of losing the friendship, but fuck, it's draining. I've wanted Ciara since the day I laid eyes on her. She's fucking gorgeous, inside and out. She puts me in the friend-zone, though. No matter what I do, no matter how many hints

I drop. She just doesn't see me. I'm tired of it, and in a sense, I guess I've given up. If a friend is all I can have her as, then that's what I'll stick with. She's always going to be my girl, but I can't keep waiting.

"Oh, Spike, I'd love to know. If she is silly enough not to snap you up, I most certainly will."

I don't get a chance to answer her, because I see Ciara standing at the top of the stairs. I turn my gaze to her, and my heart stutters. I'm not sure if it's the long, slightly curled, blonde hair, the full red lips, the porcelain skin, or the yellow eyes, but fuck, she's perfect. Her blue dress gently sways around her knees as she steps down towards us. Her eyes are on Cheyenne, and her face is filled with something I can't quite pick. It could be jealousy, or anger. I know the two of them aren't close, Ciara has told me a little bit about it. Whatever the look, it's full of emotion. When her eyes finally turn back to mine, I see a hint of betrayal.

"I see you met Cheyenne," she says, though her voice is empty.

"Yeah, I did."

"You never told me Spike was so gorgeous," Cheyenne laughs, placing a hand on my shoulder. I flinch.

"What did you call him?" Ciara asks.

"Oh, didn't you know that's what everyone calls him?"

Ciara's eyes flash with hurt, before she covers it up, and shrugs. "Well, I'm glad you two met. Are we going?"

I nod, extending my hand. Ciara reaches down and takes it, and we turn, heading for the door.

"I'll see you around, Spike. I'd love to know more about that nickname…perhaps you'll tell me all about it *next* time you're here," Cheyenne purrs again.

Well fuck. Why do I get the feeling this is going to become a complicated situation?

~*~*~*~*

PRESENT - CIARA

"Hey Tom Cat!"

I smile as Cade comes running up to me when I'm at the compound the next day. He grins, wide and beautiful, and wraps me in a hug. For a moment, I enjoy the comfort. I need it. More than I realized. He pulls back, and looks down at me, studying my face.

"You don't come here often, what's up?"

I force a smile. "I was just after Jackson."

"He's in the main bar."

"Thanks," I say, walking towards the bar. Cade falls in step beside me. "How were your few days away?"

He nods, grinning. "Fuckin' sweet. Was good to get away."

"I bet Addi had a good time?"

"Fuck yeah, she always has a good time with me. She's a fuckin' wildcat."

I shove him lightly, and he laughs.

"Get your mind out of the gutter, biker."

He wraps an arm around me. "Can't help it. The girl drives me crazy."

"Crazy is good."

He grins down at me, and then spins me around to face him. "She's inside, go and say hello to her when you're done with Jacks, yeah?"

I nod. "Yeah."

"You all good?"

I nod, forcing a smile. "I'm good."

"I'll catch you later, Tom Cat."

I watch Cade turn and walk off and then with a shake of my head, I walk inside.

The bar is quiet for a Thursday. It's usually filling up with bikers by now. Addison is at the bar, drying a batch of glasses. I wave to her when she looks up, and her eyes brighten.

I can't help the smile that stretches across my face. If anyone in the world understands pain, it's Addi. She's got a vibe about her that screams survivor, yet at the same time, it screams warmth and friendship. She's definitely someone you want in your life.

"Hey! Ciara!"

"Hey Addi," I say, walking over and stopping at the long, wooden bar. I lean my hip on it. "How's it going?"

She drops the dishcloth and sighs. "Pretty good, sick of work."

I nod in understanding. "I know what you mean, it's my first day off in ages."

"Are you getting paid again?"

I narrow my eyes. "How did you know about that?"

"Spike told Cade."

I feel my brows raise now. "Spike and Cade speak?"

"They have been, yeah. It's a slow process, but it's happening."

That makes me happy, for both of them. They deserve to find that friendship again. I imagine it would never be quite the same, but something is better than nothing at all.

"I'm happy for them," I say, fiddling with the end of the dishcloth. "And yeah, I'm getting paid again. Spike gave me some money anyway, but I'm going to give it back."

Now Addi's brows raise. "You and Spike have been talking?"

"We've been arguing more like it, but yeah...I think I hurt him the other night."

Addi turns, storming around the bar and stopping in front of me. She grips my shoulders and pulls me towards a table, shoving me down. She sits on the chair over from me, puts her elbows on the table, face in hands and leans forward. "Spill, like now."

I laugh nervously. "It's nothing, Addi. Just the usual Spike and Ciara bullshit."

"Oh, you are such a liar! Now spill, or I'll force it out of you using whatever means possible."

I giggle and roll my eyes at her, and then I lean forward too. "We've been talking a little more, and slowly we've been hashing some things out. Last night, my car ran out of gas and, well, Spike was the one who stopped for me. We got into this massive fight and he kissed me," I blurt out quickly.

Addi's eyes widen, and she grins, big and beautiful. "Spike kissed you?"

"It's not what you think. I was yelling at him because he never kissed me when he took me that night all those years ago, and so he kissed me to make it even. It meant nothing to him, I can assure you."

Addi puts her head in her hands and groans, and then she meets my gaze again. "Honey, you can't see it, can you? Spike is freakin' head over heels for you."

I snort. "No, he's not. Trust me. He might have had feelings in the past, but they're long gone now."

"Oh god! You two are so bloody stubborn. Trust me when I say his angry reaction is because he cares so much. Spike isn't the type of man to react angrily to just anyone. He's the type who reacts out of emotion and, trust me honey, he feels something when he's around you. It's why he's trying so hard to push you away."

Is Addison right? Or is she just clutching at straws to find some sort of explanation so he won't break my heart?

"Either way," I say, my voice low and croaky. "He's not about to give in anytime soon. He gave me the bracelet back; that means I hurt him. God, Addi, I said some really mean things last night."

"What bracelet?" she asks, confusion washing over her pretty features.

"A long time ago, I gave him a bracelet. It was kind of like a promise to always have each other's backs, to always be there for each other. I spat mean words at him last night and he left, but he left the bracelet on the coffee table."

"Can I be honest with you, Ciara?" Addi says, her face serious.

"Of course you can."

"Look, I know a great deal went down between you and Spike, and half of it I'll probably never know or understand but what I'm seeing here, is two people determined to blame one another for things that went wrong, yet not one of them is willing to say sorry. You're looking for Spike to take away the hurt he caused you, but what about his hurt?"

I hang my head, because she's right. Spike deserves my apology, just as much as I deserve his.

"I know you're right, but every time we get together we just end up blaming each other instead of dealing with what happened and moving on."

"Are you in love with him, honey?"

I flinch. "How can I love someone who hates me so much?"

"Easily, now answer the question."

My heart begins to hammer. I hate the question because it rips out so many emotions inside me. I can't think when she's asking me to bare my soul to her.

Once upon a time, I adored Spike. I'm fairly sure he was the first man who taught my heart how to love, even though I never admit it to him. Now, though, when I think of him, I am torn. I feel so much for him, yet at the same time my hurt overrides real feelings. I close my eyes, sucking in a rugged breath. If I admit what's in my heart, deep down behind everything, then I'm changing the way I think about everything, but if I keep it locked down...I continue on this path of denial.

"Yes."

My voice comes out as a croaky whisper. It's the best I can muster up. I clench my eyes closed harder, until they hurt. Addison will never realize what admitting that is doing to me inside. She will never realize that now I have said it, I will never walk away from it. I feel her fingers glide over my hand, and she tugs it into her grip. For a long while we just sit like that, me with my head down and eyes closed, and her holding my hand, occasionally running her thumb over it. When I finally look up, I've managed to fight the tears and am holding strong. Addison meets my gaze, and she gives me a gentle smile.

"I know how hard it is to admit you have feelings for someone like Spike, but now you've done it, you can move forward."

"There is no forward," I say in a small, broken voice. "I've fucked it all up."

"No, you haven't. You can fix this, Ciara. You just have to be willing to admit you were wrong, too."

"I still don't know if it's enough. I don't know if I can be second best..."

"You're not second best, you know that. It's not like you were both presented to him and he picked one. He thought you didn't want any more than friendship. Eventually he was going to move on and stop waiting honey, it just so happened that he moved onto your sister."

"I know…"

"Give it a few days, then try and talk to him again. Approach it differently."

I lift my hand, running it through my hair and letting out a deep sigh. "God, why can't I just find a normal man?"

Addi giggles. "They're never normal honey."

"Ciara?"

I hear Jackson's voice, and turn to see him striding into the bar. I came to apologize to him for being so rude the other night. I turn and flash Addi a quick smile, before standing and walking towards Jackson.

When we reach each other, we both stop. He gives me a smile, like my angry mood the other evening didn't bother him at all. Jackson is such a sweet man. I really don't know how he manages to run a club full of bikers.

"Hey Jackson, I just wanted to come in and apologize for the other night. It was wrong of me to snap at you like that."

He offers me his arm. "Walk with me."

I hook mine through his, and as we pass Addi, he leans down and kisses her head. She flashes him a grin and then returns to the bar.

Jackson and I walk through the halls until we reach the front door. He leads me out and we sit on a couple of old chairs beside the front door.

"You know I ain't pissed at you, Ciara?" he says, turning to face me. He rests his big hands on his knees and his green eyes meet mine.

"I know, but it was still wrong of me to behave like that all the same. I shouldn't have spoken to you like that just because I was pissed off at Spike."

He shrugs his shoulders. "You were hurtin', I can't be angry at you for that."

"I was hurt he came to you to get rid of me, like I was just a massive pain in his side, but in the end that was on him, it wasn't on you."

"Spike's in a bad place right now. He was doin' it to protect you."

"How so?" I ask, crossing my legs.

"Can't give you that kind of information, but I can tell you it wasn't out of hate that he did it."

What is Spike up to? Jackson might not be willing to tell me, but my interest is sparked.

"Either way, I'm sorry for speaking to you the way I did."

Jackson nods. "It's all good, you know we've always got your back, Ciara."

I smile. "Yeah, I know."

"Anyway," he says, standing, "I gotta run. You take care, Ciara."

I beam up at him, and he flashes me that award-winning smile before disappearing.

I sit on the chair for a long while, thinking about Jackson's words. What could Spike be up to, that would make him feel the need to keep me away so I'm protected? I would like to think Spike wouldn't put himself in danger after what happened with Cheyenne, but I wouldn't put it past him. My guess is he's seeking revenge, and, knowing Spike the way I know him.

He'll get it.

And it won't be pretty.

~*~*~*~

PAST - SPIKE

Things are going south fast, and I can't find a way to pick it all back up again. Ciara is growing cold towards me, and her sister is throwing herself at me. I know it's causing big problems between them, but fucks me if I can stop it. Ciara has had a chance, and she won't take it. Fuck, if she can't see how much I fuckin' adore her, then it's because she doesn't want to see it. If she doesn't want to see it, then what's the point in fighting to try and change it? I can't keep fighting. I'm tired of fuckin' fighting. Then Cheyenne comes along, and the girl is all over me, wanting me the way I wish her sister wanted me. I guess the selfish part of me is grateful to get a tiny piece of Ciara, even if it is through Cheyenne.

"You know," Cheyenne says as I wait out front to take Ciara to work one morning. "I'd love a ride on your bike."

"Didn't take you as the motorbike kind of girl," I say, lighting up a smoke.

"I didn't either, but if it's you I'm holding onto, I wouldn't mind."

I raise my brows, and she grins at me. Damn girl is attractive, I'll give her that much.

"Yeah, well, might have to take you for a spin."

Fuck what am I doing? I should be fuckin' walking away. I know this. Yet here I am, angry that Ciara can't see how I feel, and taking it out on her by chatting up her sister.

"How about now?"

"Can't babe, got to take Ciara to work."

"Well, how about after?" she says, stepping closer.

Fuck.

"Yeah, all right."

She beams, and it's getting to me. It's getting to me, because she's a beautiful girl and that's what happens when beautiful girls decide they want something. Ciara comes down the front stairs, and fuck, she looks good. Tight black pants, a tiny singlet, and them smokin' black boots she loves so much. Her hair is up on top of her head, in that messy thing girls do, and a pair of sunglasses covers her eyes. She's fuckin' smokin'. I don't know how she doesn't have a trail of men behind her at all times. She sees Cheyenne next to my bike, and I notice that her body stiffens. She pulls on a smile though, and walks over to me.

"Hey Danny."

"Hey Tomcat, ready?"

"I am."

She takes the helmet I hand her, and she lifts it, bringing it down over her head. Cheyenne leans in close, and fuck, she smells like some sort of sweet flower.

"I'll be here when you're done. I'm going to be waiting, don't you stand me up, Spike."

"Yeah, I'll be here."

Ciara flinches a little, but she says nothing. I pull the throttle and the bike lunges forward. Ciara wraps her tiny arms around my waist, and we ride to work. Sometimes I'm thankful that we can't speak on the bike, because I have no doubt she would have a great deal to say if she had a chance. When we pull up at the bar she's working at, she gets off the bike and pulls the helmet off. She hands it to me, and I take it, wanting to say something, but not knowing how.

"You and Cheyenne going to be seeing each other?" she asks, her voice small.

"No, I just told her I'd give her a turn on the bike, Tom Cat."

She shrugs, and that fuckin' hurts more than she'll ever know.

"It's fine, you can do whatever you want. If you want to see her, that's cool with me. I don't care."

Jesus. Could she fuckin' rip my heart out anymore?

"That what's wrong with you lately?" I ask.

"No," she says, softly. "I'm fine."

She's lying. Fuck. I want to reach out and shake her, tell her that I fuckin' want her, but there ain't no point. If she wanted to tell me she had feelings, she would have done it by now.

94

"You want me to pick you up?"

She nods. "Yeah, if you're not busy with Cheyenne."

"Tom Cat, I'm never goin' to leave you alone for anyone."

She forces that fake smile again. "Later then, Danny."

"Later, babe."

Then she's gone.

Fuck.

Why do I get the feeling I'm losing her?

CHAPTER 7

PRESENT - SPIKE

"Hey friend!"

I roll my eyes as I hear Addison's voice. I just stepped into the bar and there she is, dark hair waving about as she bounds over to me like an excited puppy. I swear to god, this girl would get under anyone's skin - she's kind of addictive. I don't smile at her, though on the inside I do. She stops in front of me, flashing me a beaming smile as she looks up, swiping a piece of stray hair from her face.

"You know you're somewhat like an annoying dog, precious?"

I don't call anyone precious, yet it seems to fit her well. She chuckles, and hooks her arm through mine.

"In a happy mood again I see?"

"Aren't I always?"

"You here to see Ciara?"

I stiffen and she stops, turning to look up at me. Devious little shit. She wanted that reaction.

"Hit a nerve?" she smirks.

I lean in close, gripping her shoulders. "Remember what I said about dancin' with wolves girl?"

"Yeah, I know, they bite and all that bullshit."

Fuckin' smart ass.

"Don't put your friend in my world, precious. You know it ain't for her."

"What I know," she says, spinning and waving down the bar attendant, "is that you aren't being very nice to her, and if you don't want her in your world, you're going the wrong way about it. Don't you know us women love a challenge?"

I grunt. "Fuckin' know it all right. Where's your old man? I'm surprised he let you out."

She laughs loudly, throwing her head back. "Yeah, well, he doesn't own me you know?"

"Does fuckin' so."

She spins around, glaring at me. "What is with you over-possessive bikers?"

"What is with you stubborn ass women?"

She narrows her eyes and turns again, ordering two beers. When she's got them in her hands, she nods towards the booth.

Well fuck, I'm not escaping her anytime soon. Funny, 'cause part of me kind of doesn't want to. Fuck, I'm turning into a pussy.

We sit down, and she slides a beer across the table at me. I grip it, take a big sip, and then put it down, staring right into her eyes.

"What's with you tryin' to push Ciara onto me?"

"What's with you being such a fucking jerk-off about it?"

I feel my lips twitch. "You need to let it go, yeah?"

"Why? Because you're being a jerk due to the fact that you care about her, or because you don't care about her?"

Fuckin' women.

"My answer to that doesn't change the fact that she's no good for me."

"Why, because of what happened with Cheyenne?"

I flinch. She continues.

"Because I imagine you don't plan on spending the rest of your life alone. If you do, that's a sad and long life you're going to have."

I narrow my eyes at her. "Your point, precious?"

"My point is that she cares about you, a lot. She's a good person, and she could be good for you, if you stopped treating her like an ass."

"That's the problem," I growl. "She's too good for me."

Addison raises her brows, and I curse inwardly. Well fuck, I just openly admitted to Addison, and a little to myself, that I don't hate Ciara and that it goes far deeper than I am willing to let on.

"Who says she's too good for you? You, or her? Because I can guarantee it doesn't matter to her what you are."

"Well it should!" I snap.

"You don't have to make the same mistakes again, Spike. You can be good to her."

"No, I fuckin' can't. Now fuckin' drop it Addison, or I'll get up and walk out."

She sighs deeply, but puts up her hands. "Fine, we'll drop it."

"Good."

We're both silent a moment, before her face brightens again and she leans forward. "You wanna do Karaoke with me?"

I raise my brows. "You fuckin' serious?"

"Oh yeah, come on, it will be fun."

"I'm a biker," I point out. "We don't fuckin' sing."

She huffs and crosses her arms. "Do you ever smile?"

"Not much."

"Well, I'll make you smile."

I raise one brow at her, and she flashes me yet another grin before taking a big sip of her beer. Then her eyes move to the corner of the room, and she brightens. She lifts her hand, waving and calling out, "Ciara!" Well fuck. I thought Ciara wasn't on tonight. Mother. Fucker.

"Hey Addi."

I hear Ciara's voice behind me, and my entire body stiffens. I can't sit here and be an absolute ass, I have to turn. So, I slowly do.

When my eyes settle on her, I want to hiss in anger. I fuckin' hate the outfits these girls dress in. More, I hate it on her because she can fuckin' rock it, and half the bar notices. Her long blonde hair is cascading down around her shoulders, and her yellow eyes fuckin' pull at my heartstrings. She places a hand on her flat, smooth belly and smiles over at Addison.

"I thought you weren't working?" Addi says.

"I wasn't meant to be, but Jenny called in sick."

"Aw, that sucks."

99

"Yeah."

"Spike, are you going to say hello?" Addison says, smirking at me.

I shoot her a truly disgusted glare, and then I look up at Ciara. "Hey."

"Hey Danny."

Fuck it. She knows it gets to me when she calls me Danny. She's the only person in the world who would still call me that, and it burns every time she does.

"Well, I'm going to get another beer," I say, standing.

"I'll get it for you," Ciara says, turning and walking towards the bar.

I flop back down onto my ass and watch her leave. That skirt really is too fuckin' short. Jesus. It puts me into a place I haven't been for a long time. It makes me want to smash every fucker that looks her way. I turn to Addison again, and she's smiling over at me.

"She has a nice ass, right?"

"Shut the fuck up Addison."

She bursts out laughing.

Fuck.

This is going to be a long night.

~*~*~*~*~

PRESENT - CIARA

His eyes are on me. Everywhere I go, they are on me. I can feel them burning into my back when I'm not facing him, and when I am they're all over me, piercing into me, saying so much, showing so much. I want him. I'm sick of denying everything that's raging between us. I hurt him. I know I did, but I'm beyond trying to figure out how I can fix him. I'm so tired of fighting.

I grip another round of drinks and walk them over to a table of young men. I can hear Addi's booming laugh across the bar, and I can't help but smile. I'm glad to see her and Spike getting along. I've even seen him crack a smile once or twice. He needs someone like her in his life, someone to just tell him how it is and take no shit.

"Hey there princess."

I spin around to see Muff leaning against the counter, grinning over at me. I smile, unable to stop myself.

"Hey Muff," I say, walking around the side of the bar and pulling out a beer. I toss it to him, and he catches it.

"Busy night?"

"You know, the usual."

"Saw your boy starin' at you. Still hasn't given in I see?"

I chuckle softly. "He's not my boy, and no, he's as stubborn as they come."

"You're tellin' me."

"What brings you to this fine bar tonight, anyway? I haven't seen you for a few days?"

He cracks open the beer and takes a long swig before putting it down onto the counter. "I came here to see a fine bar bitch…"

101

I roll my eyes at him. "Most girls would be offended by that statement, but coming from you, Muff, I think I'm flattered."

He throws his head back and laughs, causing Spike to turn in his chair and stare over at us. His eyes narrow, and I give him a quick glance, before turning back to Muff.

"You wanna know a secret, princess?" Muff says, leaning close.

"I do."

"Come closer."

I giggle. "That's kind of creepy. You're not going to kiss me are you?"

He gives me a lazy half-smile. "Would it be so bad if I did?"

"No, of course not."

I lean in and he tilts his head so his mouth is near my ear. "Prez told me to back down."

"Back down?"

"He told me to stay 'the fuck' away from you."

Spike said that? This surprises me. Maybe it's just the lifestyle he doesn't want me in, or maybe it's for his own benefit. Either way, it sends shivers up my spine. Good shivers.

"He did?"

"Oh, he did. Told me if he ever sees my lips on you again, he'll cut my dick off and feed it to me."

I raise my brows and Muff pulls back, grinning. "So go on, princess. You play him. Make it burn."

"You're a bad man, Muff."

He chuckles and lifts his beer. "Thrills me bein' bad. I'm goin' to play some pool. Check you later, little lady."

"Later Muff."

When he's gone, I can't help but swing my eyes to Spike. He's not sitting any longer, and Addi is walking over to me, a massive grin on her face. I smile back at her, wondering where Spike has disappeared to. She stops at the bar, leaning over it and placing her head in her hands.

"So, how's your night?"

I grin at her, cheeky shit. "I'm sure it's as thrilling as yours."

She winks at me, brushing a piece of long, dark hair from her eyes. "Oh, mine is totally thrilling. Spike's a hoot when he's drunk."

"Where'd he go?"

"No idea. Outside for a smoke? He's trying to ditch me. He'll never learn. I am totally not going anywhere."

I laugh. "You're like the creepy stalker friend."

"That's me, baby. Anyway, I do have to go."

I pout at her. "That sucks. I was going to have a drink with you after my shift."

"Aw, well how about you come around tomorrow? We'll have some drinks at Cade's place."

"Sounds good."

She leans over the bar and gives me a quick hug, before turning and skipping out of the bar. *That girl has far too much energy.* I couldn't keep up with her if I tried.

When she disappears out of the door, I turn and check the alcohol stock levels. We need a few more bottles so I yell out to Joe that I'm going to grab some.

I walk out back and down the hall, but I stop dead in my tracks when I see Spike standing and staring into the function room. He's just standing there, his eyes fixed on something, his body rigid. I walk over slowly, curiosity burning. I step up quietly and peer in the room. My body freezes.

There's a couple against the wall, kissing and touching. A man, with broad shoulders and long dark hair, is kissing a tiny blonde girl. His hand is cupping her breast, and her fingers are gliding up and down his backside. My eyes widen, and part of me feels so completely wrong standing here watching them. My fascination, however, is with Spike. He's breathing deeply, and is so transfixed he doesn't even realize I'm beside him yet. I know Spike likes to watch, but seeing the way his body is coming alive has mine doing the same thing. It's erotic, watching him grow hot and hard. I feel tingles break out along my skin, and my pussy begins to throb. God, why am I finding this as much of a turn on as he is? Could it just be because he's here?

"Jesus," I mutter, when the man slides his fingers down the girl's pants and she throws her head back, groaning.

Spike jerks and turns his gaze to me, but I keep my eyes on the couple. I know I shouldn't be doing this, but damn, it's doing things to my body that I've never felt before. I'm coming alive. My body is shuddering, my pussy becoming wet and ready, and my nipples are so hard they ache. Slowly, I turn my eyes to Spike, who's watching me with a look I can't quite put my finger on. Is that awe? Perhaps it's even shock. Spike probably never thought something like this would arouse me. Heck, I never thought something like this would arouse me, but here I am, wishing he would take me up against this wall and fuck me so hard I stop breathing.

"You're not turned off?" he says, his voice raspy and husky.

"Surprisingly, no. Quite the opposite actually," I breathe.

"You changed."

It's a simple statement, but it's completely true. Once upon a time, I would have found this completely wrong. Now, I can't turn myself away.

"I guess I did."

He makes a hissing sound when the man drops to his knees, lifting the girl's foot and placing it on his shoulder. Then his face is in her pussy, tongue sliding over her clit. Shit. I need to walk away. Like, now. All this sexual tension makes me need to pee. Odd, I know but my lower half is in uproar right now.

"I need to relieve myself," I whisper, turning away.

Spike turns to me, his expression completely shocked. It takes me a moment to realize what I said sounds very…well…wrong.

"No," I laugh nervously. "I meant I need to pee."

"Right," he says, shaking the shock from his body.

As I go to turn, reality hits me hard. Spike and I just spoke without argument, and better, we found common ground. For a moment, just for a small moment, we weren't tearing each other's heads off. Deciding to risk it, I turn back to Spike and meet his heated gaze.

"Hey Spike?"

His eyes scan my face before he rasps, "Yeah?"

"Do you want to have a drink with me?"

His brows shoot up, and that shock returns to his face. For a moment he looks like he might not answer. I know he's already had a fair bit to drink, and maybe that's why it's different, but he surprises me by saying, "Yeah, Tom Cat. That'll be sweet."

I nod at him, and then turn and walk to the toilets. Once I'm in, I lean against the door and take a deep, shaky breath. This could be it for us; this moment could be the one that changes everything. I can't stuff it up. If anything, I want the chance to slowly recreate our friendship. We both deserve that much.

I quickly relieve myself, and give my face a wash before heading back out to the bar. Spike's sitting at it, so I walk over and open a beer, handing it to him. He grins at me. It's not a full grin, but it's so god damned beautiful it takes my breath away.

"I'm just about finished," I say. "Do you mind hanging for a few?"

Spike shakes his head. "Nah, all good."

For a moment, that awkward silence just hangs around. I don't really know what to talk about. What can I say that won't start an argument? I can't speak about my sister, I can't speak about the club and I can't speak about the past. Dammit, why do things always have to be so complicated? Why can't we just have that easygoing, fun, light friendship we used to have? Maybe I'm trying too hard. Perhaps the trick is to just stop trying.

"How long you plannin' on stayin' here?"

I'm shocked by Spike's question, and even more shocked he spoke first.

"Here, as in this town?"

He nods, sipping his beer and letting those gorgeous eyes scan my face, looking for a reaction.

"Until I have enough money to go to college."

He tilts his head to the side, still studying me closely. "Never knew you wanted to study, Tom Cat."

God I love it when he calls me that. It sends warmth right through my body.

"I do, I was always planning on going but…"

"But Cheyenne died and you ran off, making your parents cut your trust fund."

I swallow and nod. "Yeah, something like that."

"Ain't a bad thing to have to work for what you want. Makes it that much better in the end."

I nod, picking up a glass and drying it. "You're right about that."

"Do you still talk to them?"

I shake my head, swallowing again. "No, I haven't for months."

"Is that 'cause of me?"

"It's not just you, Spike, it's everything. It's how they treated me long before you came into the picture."

"They never did treat you the same as her, did they?"

I meet his gaze, and for a moment I see pure compassion in those brown depths. Did Spike see all the times my parents favored her over me?

"Yeah, well, I wasn't as smart as Cheyenne. I didn't have the looks. I didn't have the personality. She was their angel, I was the accident."

"Not to me you weren't."

His words hit me hard, and I struggle for a moment, to breathe. *Not to me you weren't.* God, what is that supposed to mean? Before I can answer, Joe walks over, tapping me on the shoulder.

"You can go love, it's settled down in here."

I turn, struggling to gather my emotions. "Thanks Joe, I'll see you tomorrow."

With shaky hands, I turn to Spike. "You want to stay here?"

He shakes his head. "Nah, you wanna go for a drive?"

Oh god, yes, yes.

"I'll get my things."

I turn and rush out the back, changing out of my work uniform into a light, summer dress. I let my hair out, running my fingers through it, then I grip my purse and keys before heading back out. Spike is just purchasing a pack of beer for us, and when he turns, our eyes meet and electric bolts spread through my body. For the first time in a long time, I wonder if Spike and I might actually have a decent conversation.

"Ready?" he asks.

"Yeah, ready."

We head out the front doors and over to my little car. Spike jumps in the front seat and I get into the driver's side. I start the car, turn on the cooling, and then I pull out onto the road.

My heart is thudding, and my head is spinning. Spike is in my car, with me, willingly. I don't want to stuff this up. I want a chance to talk to him, to move on from this tension that's constantly between us. This is my chance; this is the only one I might have.

"I wanted to say I'm sorry about the other night. The way I spoke to you wasn't fair. I just want us to be friends, even for a night. Can we do that? Can we go somewhere tonight and just be Ciara and Danny again. For one night, can we just get along?"

Spike turns to me, and I can see him watching me from the corner of his eye. "Yeah, Tom Cat, that would be good."

"Anywhere you want to go?" I ask, my voice shaky.

"Yeah, to the local lake."

My heart thuds. When we were younger, we used to spend a lot of time at the lakes. We didn't live here when we were growing up, but the fact that he wants to take me to a lake, means the world to me.

"Sounds good."

We drive down to the lake, and it's quiet. No one is around, and the only light is the full moon shining down over the water. Spike and I get out of the car and find a spot under a large oak tree. We sit against the massive trunk, and Spike pulls out the beers, handing me one. We stare out at the water for a long, long moment before he finally speaks.

"Remember when you threw yourself down that hill when you saw a snake?"

I huff and laugh softly. "Yeah, that hurt like hell."

"Fuckin' funniest day of my life."

"Yeah, well, it was funny after…"

He grins and turns to me. Oh that grin, that devastating grin. I smile back, unable to stop the curl from transforming my face.

"Tell me about your life, Tom Cat. Tell me what happened while I wasn't in it."

I sigh deeply, and take a long pull of the bitter beer.

"Not much to tell. I lived with Mom and Dad for a long while. Things were bad, so I moved up here. Cade and Jackson helped me out, and I started working. I stayed with them until I could afford my own place and since then I have just been working to get enough money for school."

"No man then?"

"There was one."

"What happened?" he asks, pulling out a cigarette and offering me one.

"No thanks," I say.

He lights the cigarette, and then leans against the trunk again. "Well?"

"He just wasn't…for me. We were together a little while, things were okay, but it was just never there you know? That spark."

"Yeah, I'm hearin' ya."

"After that, I just kept to myself."

"Tom Cat's been dry?" he jokes lightly.

"Something like that." I laugh.

"You know, for what it's worth, I am sorry you came back to find me married."

I flinch and he stares at me, our eyes just holding each other's for what seems like minutes.

"I know you are."

He looks away, and his shoulders straighten. "It was better that way."

"For who?"

"For you."

"How do you suppose that is?"

He turns back to me. "I was never good enough for you, Tom Cat. Cheyenne, she was easy, she was flirty and outgoing. You were different, you were beautiful, quiet, and fuckin' fragile. I would have broken you."

"That was my problem," I say in a soft, small voice. "I was never enough to compare."

He spins to me, gripping my arm. "You were more than enough, that was the fuckin' problem. You more than compared. You were very different to her, but it wasn't in a way that made you any less beautiful."

I swallow, and my body winds up tightly with tension.

"Cade told me…he told me you had feelings for me."

Spike flinches. "Long time ago, Tom Cat."

"You didn't tell me."

He narrows his eyes. "You didn't tell me either."

"No, I guess I didn't. I wanted to, but then Cheyenne came in and you took a liking to her, so I didn't bother."

"I went to her, and I fell in love with her, but she wasn't what I wanted for myself, Tom Cat. I wanted you, but you wouldn't give me a god damned inch."

"You didn't think of telling me?" I snap, crossing my arms. "You didn't think that maybe you should have said something before you just ran off with Cheyenne?"

"What was the fuckin' point? You couldn't fuckin' see it. I tried, fuck knows I tried, and yet you didn't see me. I was sick of tryin'. Cheyenne threw herself on me, and I thought what the fuckin' heck?"

I feel my body begin to shake. "I didn't see it, Spike. It wasn't because I didn't want to, it was because I was so scared I would ruin everything if you knew how I felt."

"Fuck, Ciara, I was constantly with you. I picked you up every motherfuckin' day, I spent every motherfuckin' weekend with you, I was there all the time."

"I know that!" I cry. "God, Spike, I know you were, okay? I didn't see it. I was young and I didn't fucking see it. Then she came along and I stopped believing there was a chance. It wasn't just on me, or you, it was on us both. We both walked away without telling each other there was so much more to it. I know what I gave up, I know I passed you over to her and I regret it every day."

"I don't regret it, Tom Cat. I loved Cheyenne, and I don't regret marrying her...bu—"

I get to my feet, hurt. His words are something I already know, but it's the way he says them. He grips my arm before I can spin away, and yanks me back down. I land harshly, and attempt to slap his hand away, but his grip is too strong.

"One fucking moment," I spit. "One fucking moment can't go by without her being better. One fucking moment, I'd like to mean a tiny bit more than her. You can't fucking see it, can you? You walk around with those stupid fucking rose-colored glasses on, unable to see anything she did. I never doubted you loved her Spike, I knew you did. I saw it. I lived it. But for one fucking moment I wish it was me."

I jerk my hand out of his grip, and spin, turning to walk off.

"It was you," he yells, stopping me in my tracks. "I don't regret her, Ciara. Not for a fuckin' second. I don't regret lovin' her, I don't regret marryin' her. Cheyenne changed my life, she changed a part of me, but you, Ciara, were the one who opened my heart. You were the first one to claim it and you were the one who fuckin' tore it out of my chest the day you ran off. You never gave me a motherfuckin'

113

chance to explain myself to you. I woke up after we slept together and you were gone. Couldn't fuckin' find you. It was you who took my heart, and you who fuckin' broke it. She picked the pieces up when I couldn't find you, and so I stopped fighting. Cheyenne might have had me in the end, Tom Cat, but my heart was always yours first."

Hot tears spill out of my eyes, and my knees wobble. Slowly, I lower myself to the ground. Spike puts his beer down, and crawls over to me. He stops in front of me, reaching up to grip my face. He tilts it up towards me, and gently, his thumb swipes away my tears.

"Fuck, Ciara, you just can't see that you meant the motherfuckin' world to me."

"Then why do you hate me so much now?"

"Don't fuckin' hate you," he growls, his voice low and raspy. "I'm tryin' to protect you, and all it's doin' is makin' me need you more. Walk away from me, Tom Cat. Do yourself a favor, and run. I ain't ever gonna be what you need. Ain't ever gonna be what anyone needs. Why can't you just see that?"

"Running is for people who don't have the balls to fight," I whisper, leaning in close to him, breathing in his scent. Tonight it's a mix; I can smell beer as well as that musky scent that is his alone.

"When are you gonna see there's no point in fightin' for something that don't wanna be fought for?"

"I won't, because everyone deserves to be fought for Spike. Even you."

"Fuck," he growls. "Just fuckin' stop makin' me want you. I am not what you need, can't you see that?"

"No," I rasp, leaning in closer.

"Tom Cat, this is playin' with fuckin' fire. You'll get burned."

"I'll risk it."

I grip his shirt and pull him forward, and without protest he comes. His lips crash down over mine and everything inside me comes to life. I don't give a fuck about the past, the future or what's going to happen tomorrow. All I care about is right now, this moment, with him. He growls, reaching up and tangling his fingers into my hair. He jerks my head, bending it back so he can deepen the kiss. He sweeps his tongue through my mouth, tangling it with mine and causing ripples to run through my body. I want Spike; I want him inside me, deep and hard. It's where he should have always been. It's where I want him to remain.

I wrench my mouth away from his, and tangle my fingers in his shirt. "Fuck me, Spike. I want you to fuck me."

"Tom Cat," he growls, letting his eyes slide over me. "That ain't a fuckin' good idea."

"Fuck what it ain't, I want it, and I want it now."

"Shit."

I don't let him go on; I pull him back, connecting his lips with mine again. From that moment, things suddenly become frantic. My body is pushed down onto the grass, and Spike is looming over me, his big, hard body, flush against mine. I can feel every inch of him, every delicious, firm inch. His cock pulses against my belly and his lips are all over me, running down my neck, over my jaw and occasionally stopping to engage in a deep, intense kiss that has my head spinning.

His fingers slide up my belly slowly. He slips them under my shirt and up until he finds my bra. He grips it, lifting it up to expose my breasts. He takes hold of my nipples in his thumb and forefinger and I arch, rasping out his name as he begins to roll them. He growls against my neck, and leans his head down, replacing his finger with his mouth. The warmth of his lips as he encloses them around my nipple is enough to take my breath away. I cry out, thrusting my hips up and grinding against his cock, desperate for him, desperate for release.

"Fuckin' sweet tits babe, fuckin' sweetest tits I ever fuckin' put my lips on."

I groan, thrashing my head from side to side. His free hand slips up and under my skirt, skimming his fingertips over my damp panties.

"So fuckin' wet for me baby, so fuckin' sweet."

He runs his fingers up and down the silk, teasing me, taunting me. I whimper, gripping his back and taking hold of his jacket, sliding his colors off. He moves, taking his fingers from my panties to toss the jacket to the side. I grip his shirt, bringing him back down and sliding my fingers up underneath it, feeling the warmth of his firm, taut back. His skin quivers as I slide my fingers up and down, gently grazing him with my nails.

His fingers are back at my panties, and he slides them aside, sliding two fingers inside to find my damp, throbbing sex. Growling, he rubs his fingertips over my clit, causing me to jerk and cry out. God I need him. Now. Hard and fast.

"Don't wanna wait," I whimper. "Spike, I want to fuck you."

"Babe, I know, hush."

He slips one finger down, and into my pussy. I arch, stretching around him, clenching as he slides his finger out, and plunges it back in.

"So fuckin' tight, baby, you're so fuckin' ready for my cock."

"Yes," I cry out, tilting my hips up, taking more of him.

He gently drives his fingers in and out, in and out, until I'm on the edge, until my body wants to come so badly I'm shaking.

"Look at me, Tom Cat. Watch me with those fuckin' beautiful eyes when you come around my finger. Fuckin' watch me."

I stare up at him, and my vision begins to cloud as my orgasm begins, ripping through my body like wildfire. I open my mouth, and cry out hoarsely. Spike growls, never moving his eyes from mine as he gently slows his fingers, wringing out every, last shudder from my body. The moment I stop shuddering, he slips his fingers from me, and lifts them to my mouth.

"Suck them baby, show me how much you fuckin' love the way I make you come."

I open my mouth, and he slips his fingers inside. I wrap my lips around them, and I suck gently, swirling my tongue, tasting my own release. Spike's eyes cloud over and he gives me a hooded expression.

"Fuck, yes…"

He slides his fingers from my mouth, and then lifts himself to his knees. He grips his jeans, unbuttoning them and lowering them. His large cock strains against his boxers, and I swallow, my heart beginning to thump as anticipation gets the better of me. So long I've dreamt of feeling Spike inside me again.

He grips the top of his boxers and pulls them down, and there it is…God, that cock. It's large, throbbing and shiny. The piercings in his cock run up the entire length so when it stands on end, it looks like a lineup of bowties. Each barbell has a spike on the end, and they meet one large piercing straight through the eye of his dick. The spikes on that piecing are the biggest.

Spike runs his hands up and down his cock, and it takes me a moment to realize what he's doing. He's pulling off the spikes. I've always been curious as to how he works the piercings, but when I see him removing just the ends, I realize the spikes are just clip-ons. He runs his fingers up and down, sexily removing each spike, until all that's left are round barbells in their place. The piercings glisten under the moonlight, and I swallow. Fuck, now I know why they would be so erotic to remove. I lick my lips thinking about being on my knees in front of him, nipping off each spike, sucking his hard length as I went. Jesus, it's not a wonder women love it.

Spike drops the pointy tips into his pocket, and then he pulls out a condom, rolling it over his length as he watches me, his eyes hooded and lusty. When he's sheathed, he shifts out of his jeans and drops down over the top of me. His mouth finds mine, hot and desperate, and my fingers go up to grip his hair. I tug the thick locks, bringing his mouth down over mine so hard my lips burn. He slides a hand down my leg, gripping my thigh and lifting it over his hip. His fingers reach down and slip my panties aside, and something about that has my body coming to life. It's so dirty, and quick, and fucking erotic. Then he's pressing against me, his hard cock probing my entrance. I groan and wrap my other leg around him, encouraging him down. I want him now. Inside me. All over me. Everywhere.

He gently pushes the head in, and the sensational feeling of burning and pleasure that shoots through my body is what I've been waiting for all these years. I close my eyes and drop my head back onto the grass. His lips find my throat as he pushes in, stretching and filling me until he's in so deep, his balls rub gently against my ass. We both growl, raw and primal. He jerks his hips, sliding his length out and slamming it back in. I can feel every one of those piercings, rubbing against me, stirring those sensitive nerves inside my body. My nails scrape against his scalp as I tighten my grip in his hair, arching my back to offer him my exposed nipple.

"So fuckin' dirty baby, you're fuckin' beautiful."

He closes his lips over my nipple and picks up his pace, thrusting deep and hard, slapping against me and driving into me desperately. My legs are around his waist, my hands in his hair, my mouth on his neck, licking the salty slickness off as he picks up the pace, bringing me to the edge. No man, god, not one, has ever brought me this close to the edge so quickly. Spike's cock works me, his body works mine, his lips cause me to drown, to forget, to just feel. I feel him. All of him. Every god damned beautiful inch. I teeter on the edge of orgasm, my body shaking violently as I inch closer and closer with each, hard thrust.

"Come for me Tom Cat, fuckin' come around my cock."

"God, Spike, yes."

"Say my name baby, fuckin' say it."

"Spike," I rasp.

"No, the other one. Say my real name," he growls, thrusting harder.

"Danny," I scream, my orgasm tearing through me like liquid fire. "God, Danny."

"Yes, fuck, yes," he roars, thrusting harder and harder until he's joining me in release.

His body jerks, and he throws his head back, growling loudly as his cock begins to pulse inside me. I clench and squeeze, shuddering and crying out as we both wring each other dry.

His body slumps down on mine, and his damp forehead rests on my chest. We're both breathing heavily, our bodies still trembling. I take his head, wrapping my fingers around it and holding him close for a few moments. When we're both able to move, he rolls over and lands on the grass, taking me into his arms. I stare up at the stars, for the moment, completely content.

"Fuck, Tom Cat. You changed."

"You said that already," I whisper.

"Yeah, but fuck…didn't realize how much it was goin' to change this…"

"What's this?" I say, swallowing.

"Don't fuckin' know, kid."

Neither did I.

That was the scary thing.

CHAPTER 8

PAST - CIARA

Danny spins me, and my yellow summer dress flicks out. I squeal, tightening my arms around his neck. His laugh fills my ears, and the music pulses through my body. I feel so alive - everything is just so light and easy.

Danny and I have been dancing for the last two hours, twirling and laughing like two teenagers. It's our friend, Sally's, twenty-first birthday, and so we joined her at her fifties dress up party. Danny places me on my feet, and I spin happily. I grip his shoulders, grinning up at him. He looks gorgeous in his suit. It's not something you would expect to see Danny wearing, and yet he manages to pull it off perfectly.

"Need another drink, Tom Cat. You want one?" he says, staring down at me with those deep, brown eyes.

"Please."

He winks at me and turns, walking off into the crowd. I smile at his back, and then I spin on my heel and run straight into my sister. I yelp and leap backwards.

"Jesus, Cheyenne, why do you sneak up on me like that?"

She laughs softly, and waves her hand. I can tell by the way she's swaying, that she's well on her way to being extremely drunk. Her hair is curled and the tiny, flared, black dress she's wearing barely covers her underwear.

"Where's Spike?"

I hate that she calls him that. Like she knows something about him that I don't. Something that he won't share with me. It burns me, deep to my very core, because he won't let me see the side of him I know she's seen: the hard, rugged, side that is so clearly in there.

"He's getting a drink, and his name is Danny."

She giggles. "Not what he told me."

"Why are you trying so hard to get his attention anyway?" I ask, swiping some damp hair from my forehead.

Cheyenne has been determined to get close to Danny from the moment she met him. Her claws are out, and she's not backing down.

"Why does it matter to you? I thought you two were only friends? Or maybe you're jealous because you want him for yourself…"

"We are just friends!" I say quickly. "I don't care what you do. If you want him, go for it. I don't have feelings for Danny."

I hate that I've said those words the moment they leave my lips. I hate them because they're not true. I've wanted to be with Danny since the moment I met him, and every second I spend with him that want only gets stronger. I don't push, though, because it's clear he doesn't see me as anything more than a friend. I don't want to ruin what we've created by throwing myself at him. He's far too important to me. Yet saying those words to Cheyenne, and watching her smirk grow, makes me wish I had the balls to throw myself at him and take a chance. That's not me though; I don't take chances. That's my problem.

"Here's your drink."

I hear Danny's voice, and I pray that he didn't hear me practically tossing him at my sister. I turn, and smile as I take the drink. His eyes aren't as playful as they were when he walked off. I swallow, horrified that I could be so careless. Friends or not, I basically just gave my sister permission to take him for herself.

Cheyenne turns when she notices him, and takes a step forward, stopping in front of him and flashing a winning smile. She stretches her fingers out, and runs them down the front of his gray suit. He meets her gaze for a long, heated moment. I swallow and pain rips through my body.

"Hey, Spike. Fancy a dance?"

Danny turns his eyes to mine, and for a long moment he stares at me. It's like he's giving me a chance to say no, to pull him back and tell him I never want his hands on another woman. That the idea of anybody else touching him burns me so badly I can hardly breathe.

I say nothing, though. I can't. I don't want to be the girl who falls in love with her best friend, and ruins what they've created. I don't want him to turn to me, and wonder why I ever opened my mouth and caused a problem between us.

No, I won't be that girl. Danny is my friend, and I love him more than he'll ever know, and unless I know for sure he feels the same, then he'll never find out what my heart wants.

I'm sure I see a flash of pain in his eyes, but he quickly covers it with a hard, sexy expression. He turns to Cheyenne and grins down at her, his smile wide and alluring. Something inside me dies a little. And fuck, it's my fault. Every moment of pain I feel is on me.

"I'd love a dance," he purrs, taking her hand and turning her, leading her to the dance floor.

That's it for me. That was the one moment in life, when you get a chance to change everything for yourself and you don't take it.

I didn't take my moment.

My moment just walked away from me.

And somehow I knew, right there, standing in the middle of the dance floor…that I wouldn't get my moment back.

CHAPTER 9

PRESENT - SPIKE

I roll, and the hot, tiny body beside me groans and moves. I open my eyes, and blink over and over until they're not blurred any longer. The first thing I see is the blonde hair spread out over my pillow: thick, beautiful, blonde hair that smells like fuckin' vanilla. I let my eyes slide down, and I sigh deeply. Motherfucker. *Ciara.*

My gaze rakes her naked body; perfect little tits swelling out over the top of my sheets. Long, lean neck that's covered in my marks. Marks I made while I was fuckin' balls deep inside her. Her large, pretty fuckin' lips are parted, and she's breathing deeply.

Fuck.

Fuck.

Fuck.

What the fuck have I done? I've fucked the one girl I swore I'd never fuck again. I swore I'd stay away. Swore I'd fucking keep my hands off her and yet she's here, in my bed, sleepin' soundly after I buried myself in her all night. Fuck.

I'm such a fuckin' idiot. I should have stayed away, but then last night happened. She saw me watchin' that couple, and she fuckin' liked it. Her cheeks flushed, her body got hot, and she was lookin' at me like she wanted to fuckin' eat me alive. I should have walked away then. That was the moment I should have turned, but here I am...and now I don't want to fuckin' walk away. I want her. I *need* her. I don't want any other fucker touchin' her, and that scares the fuck outta me.

'Cause it ain't fuckin' right.

She shouldn't be here.

Another groan and she rolls. Fuck. I get out of the bed, jerking on a pair of boxers and creeping outta the room like a fuckin' freak.

I head down the hall and into the kitchen. Granger is standing at the counter, smoking, as always. He raises his brows when I come out, and I give him a 'Don't fuckin' say a word' kind of expression. He grins at me. Fuckin' asshole.

"Busy night, Prez?"

"Somethin' like that," I growl, pulling out a cigarette and bringing it to my lips, lighting it.

"That bitch you got in there can scream. Fuck me, kept me awake all night."

Fuck.

Fuck.

Fuck.

I glare at him, and he puts his hands up. "Special one?"

"Ciara," I grunt.

"I'm fuckin' sorry, what did you say?"

Here we fuckin' go.

"I said, it's Ciara."

He slowly lowers his cigarette, crushing it out before looking up at me with fierce eyes.

"Are you fuckin' brain-dead?"

"No, I'm fuckin' not."

"What the fuck have you been fightin' for? You've been bustin' your balls tryin' to keep her away for weeks, and now you're divin' balls deep into her? Fuck, Prez, what the fuck is wrong with you?"

I spin on him, leaning close and clenching my fists. "Shut your fuckin' mouth. I don't have to answer to any of you fuckers. My business is just that, fuckin' mine."

"It ain't just your business, Prez. It's all of us you're puttin' at risk. Involvin' her in this shit, it's fuckin' bad."

"She ain't gettin' involved!" I bark. "She's protected by the Knights, and she ain't got shit to do with what's goin' down."

"It's dangerous!"

I clench my fists. "She ain't gonna be involved."

"You're playin' with fuckin' fire, Prez. You want to lose another woman to fuckin' Hogan?"

"No I fuckin' don't," I bellow, slamming my fist onto the counter. "I don't want her to have anything to do with that sorry son of a bitch, but I can't fuckin' tie her up and force her away from me. I fuckin' tried, Granger. I fuckin' tried, but she ain't takin' no for an answer. Best option for me right now is to keep her fuckin' close to make sure she's safe."

Granger studies me for a long moment, and then shakes his head.

"Fuck, Prez…"

"What?" I growl.

"You fuckin' love the bitch."

"Call her a motherfuckin' bitch again, I'll cut your fuckin' dick off and shove it up your ass."

"Didn't answer my question," he snorts, lighting another cigarette.

"Nothing to fuckin' answer. I don't love, and I sure as shit ain't gettin' another woman killed. I'm enjoyin' her, keepin' her safe while that prick is on the streets. After that, it's done."

"Whatever you say, Prez."

I glare at him, but can't say another word because I hear the floorboards squeak, and turn to see Ciara walkin' out. Fuck. Well *fuck*. She's wearing one of my shirts and it just barely covers her sweet ass. Her hair is flowing down around her shoulders, and she looks like a tiny fuckin' pixie. She turns those yellow eyes to mine and I shudder, yeah, fuckin' *shudder*. I want her again. My cock burns to be buried deep inside her again.

This shit ain't good. It ain't how it was meant to go, and yet I fuckin' can't turn away. I want to run my fingers across those sweet, full cheeks and slide my tongue across those full, sweet as sugar lips.

"Hey," she whispers, letting her eyes slide over me, then she gives Granger a quick glance.

I catch his expression; it's shocked. His brows are raised and he's standing straight now, instead of leaning against the counter.

"Hey, Tom Cat," I husk.

"I…woke and didn't know where I was for a minute. I couldn't find my clothes."

Her cheeks just flushed. Motherfucker.

"Got 'em."

"Right," she whispers. "Well, um, can I have them? I have to work."

"Yeah, babe, I'll take you."

I give Granger a warning look, before turning and walking towards Ciara. She flushes deeper, and I have to grip my boxers and adjust my fuckin' cock so she won't see how badly I want her. Fuck this want. Been fightin' this want for fuckin' years and now she's pullin' it outta me, and I can't turn her away.

I don't have it in me anymore. I can't say no. I don't want to fuckin' say no, even thought I should. I should be tellin' her to leave, tellin' her it was a great fuckin' night but it ain't goin' to be happening again. But I'm not goin' to say that.

I'm fucked.

~*~*~*~*

PRESENT - CIARA

Jesus, he's looking at me like he wants to eat me alive. And I want him to. Again and again.

I turn on my heel, cursing my flushing cheeks as I walk back toward his room. I can hear him behind me, padding down the hall, no doubt thinking about last night. *I* can't stop thinking about last night. He fucked me four times, and each time was better than the

129

last. His body, his mouth, his hands, everything about him had me drowning in my own fucking pleasure. He made me feel, and god, it's been so long since I've felt anything.

When we step into his room, I try to keep my eyes off his body—his ripped, large, tattooed body that is all I can see right now. Lazily, my gaze slides down over his hard chest and taut abs. I stop at his cock straining in his loose boxers and shit, I want to get on my knees and suck him until he's growling my name and coming, hot and hard, in my mouth. I step forward, not even realizing I'm moving until I am just about flush against him. His eyes grow hooded as he looks over me. *Damn, just damn.* I stretch my fingers out, grazing them over his chest.

"Babe, I would love to be buried in you right now, but there's no fuckin' way I'm putting my cock inside you again. I'll leave you raw and not fuckin' walkin'."

I don't care.

I want to be raw.

"Don't care," I whisper.

"I care," he says, gripping my chin and tilting my face up. "And you gotta go to work."

This is it. He's going to send me on my way with a poor excuse as to why he can't continue seeing me. My eyes burn and I turn my face away, ashamed that yet again, I'm going to have to walk away from him. I spin, not wanting him to see the tears glistening in my eyes.

"Hey," he says, his voice rough. "What the fuck?"

I don't look back, I just lean down and grip my purse. "I get it," I say. 'If you want me to leave, Spike, just say so. I didn't expect anything more from you."

Silence.

I slowly turn to see him staring at me, arms crossed, body rigid. "That all you fuckin' think of me, huh? You think I'm just goin' to fuck you and get rid of you?"

Wait. What?

"Aren't you?" I say, my voice small.

"Nah, I fuckin' wasn't. I was savin' your sweet ass, because if I shoved my cock inside you once more, you'd tear in fuckin' two. Don't mean I don't wanna fuck you again, 'cause it's all I can fuckin' think about. As usual though, you fuckin' decide you know me better than I know myself and jump to conclusions before I get a chance to speak."

Shit.

"I…"

"Get your fuckin' ass over here."

"But…"

His eyes grow heated. "Don't fuckin' argue, Ciara. Get in front of me. Now."

"I didn't mean to…"

"Ciara," he growls. "Here. Now."

Slowly, I begin walking toward him. I stop in front of his large, powerful form and peer up at him through a curtain of hair that has

fallen over my eyes. He tangles his fingers in that hair, and moves it aside so our eyes are connected.

"You've had a lot to fuckin' say to me over the past few weeks, and you've hardly let me get a fuckin' word in. I'm goin' to get my word in now. The past was fucked up, but the good thing about the past is that's just what it is…it's over, it's finished.

"I made a lot of fuckin' mistakes. One of those was never tellin' you how I felt. You're a stubborn, bull-headed woman and you can't seem to take no for an answer, and it drives me fuckin' bat shit crazy - but I can't get enough of you. I don't want to turn you away, even though I know it's the best fuckin' thing for you. Ain't my place to choose who you fuckin' love, and it sure as shit ain't my place to decide how you see me.

"I can't give you sweet things, and I can't promise you nothin'. I've got a dangerous life, and until that life is sorted, I ain't takin' you as my Old Lady. I am gonna take you though, every fuckin' night and day, 'cause you belong in my bed.

"Now, you get a choice here. You can turn and walk out that door and let me go for good, or you can hang onto me, knowin' that right now I can't give you everything you want, but knowin' that one day, that might change."

Oh god. Those words, they're what I've needed for so long. They're everything I've been waiting for. I know Spike can't promise me things, and I know right now I can't be a great deal more than a good time, but fuck, I'm *his* good time and that's fine by me. I throw myself at him, slamming into his body and sending us both stumbling backwards. With a grunt, he wraps his arms around me and pulls me close, crushing our bodies together until I can hardly breathe, but oh, I don't care. I reach up, gripping his face and bringing his lips down over mine. He kisses me with need. With want. With desperation. With everything we want to say, but can't.

"That a fuckin' yes?" he growls, wrenching his lips from mine.

"It's a fuckin' yes."

He chuckles, and leans down close again. "You little fuckin' ripper."

Damn.

Just *damn*.

CHAPTER 10

PRESENT - SPIKE

"You fuckin' sure about this?" Cade asks, dropping a cigarette and crushing it out with his boot.

I glare at him. This fucker doesn't get a say in what I do right now. He don't get a fuckin' say in my life at all. He's here, because I need him. He owes me and he knows it.

I hate havin' to use him, but I don't get much of a choice. He's the only one I have right now who can back me up if my boys get in the shit. We've got an unspoken agreement, and our clubs don't have any problems with each other. *Yet.*

I light another cigarette. Fuck, I need to stop smoking. Honest to fuckin' god, it'll be this that kills me, I'm almost sure of it.

Cade narrows his eyes at me, I know what he's thinking, but he's not going to argue too heavily about it. He wouldn't fuckin' dare.

"I know what I'm doin'," I growl at him. "Now you're either with me, or you ain't, but I will be fuckin' doin' this."

"I have no fuckin' doubt about that, Spike, but you need to be thinkin' this through."

"Fuckin' have," I snarl. "And it's the best option."

"This goes wrong again…"

"It won't," I bellow, storming toward him and gripping his shirt in my fists. I jerk him so hard his jaw snaps together. "You need to shut your fuckin' mouth and decide if you're on my side or not. If you are, then you do as I say; if you're not, then fuck off."

He grips my wrists, clenching them in his hands. I grind my teeth but don't let go. "Get your fuckin' hands off me," he snaps. "And if you ever fuckin' touch me again, I'll bury you."

I drop my hands and he shoves me, hard. I'm about to lunge back at him, when Granger comes out of the warehouse and gives me a stiff shake of the head. Fuck. I take a step back, giving Cade a look that tells him I won't be takin' his fuckin' shit. He returns that look with fire in his eyes.

"You two need to fuckin' back down. We got shit goin' down and your heads need to be in the game," Granger barks, stepping in between us.

"Fuckin' hearin' ya, Granger," Cade growls.

"Yeah, me too," I hiss.

"Well, then you two need to fuckin' stop bangin' heads and maybe try puttin' them together. We need to figure out how to approach Hogan and his gang lookin' for drugs. If they get suspicious, fuck, if they even come close to getting suspicious, we're fucked."

"That's why we're sendin' Cade's boy in," I say, taking a long pull of my cigarette.

"You found out how to contact him yet?" Granger asks.

"No, that's where Cade's guy comes in. We found some links to Hogan. Cade's boy is going to approach him, lookin' for the crack Hogan sells. He'll get through eventually, and when he does, he'll give us a location."

"And if that doesn't work?"

I step up to Granger. "It'll fuckin' work."

"You got protection for your girl while this shit is goin' down?"

I flinch, and I see Cade's eyes flare. Fuckin' *fuck*. Cade doesn't know about Ciara and I.

"No," I grind out, "haven't done that yet."

"What girl?" Cade asks, his voice icy.

"That Ciara chick," Granger says, completely unaware that he is digging my fuckin' grave.

"What?" Cade snarls.

"None of your business, Cade," I say, giving him a look filled with warning.

He's in front of me before I can blink. His large hands wrap around my throat, and he squeezes. All the air leaves my lungs and I struggle to pull anymore in. The cigarette in my fingers drops to the ground.

"You piece of motherfuckin' shit, you stay the fuck away from Ciara. She ain't gonna end up some whore on your belt. She's better than that, and fuck, she's better than you. I won't let you kill another woman because of your motherfuckin' stupid mistakes."

I deck him.

Hard.

My fist swings up, and hits him so hard in the jaw his head swings sideways. An almighty crack fills the area, and blood spurts from Cade's lip. His hands leave my throat, and his fist finds my

136

eye, which splits, and blood pours down my face. My head throbs and I roar in pain, gripping my face. I turn, lunging at Cade.

Granger jumps between us, and pulls out his gun, pointing it toward me. I skid to a halt and my eyes flare as I pant with anger, desperate to get my hands on Cade.

"Fuckin' back down, Prez. Ain't worth this shit. Walk away."

"You fuckin' piece of shit, Spike," Cade bellows from behind Granger. "She's too fuckin' good for you."

"She wanted it!" I snarl. "You hear me? She fuckin' wanted it. She's been chasin' me!"

"I'll fuckin' gut you!"

Granger spins around, pointing the gun at Cade. "You're on our territory now, and no one is goin' to speak to Prez like that. Get on your fuckin' Harley and leave, Cade. We'll be in contact."

Cade, who is panting, knows the rules when it comes to other MCs. His eyes meet mine, and so many things pass between us.

"You fuckin' stay outta her life, Spike."

Then he turns and storms out of the compound. I curse, and lift my fingers, swiping the blood from my busted eye. Granger turns to me, tucking his gun in his pants.

"He's fuckin' right. Seein' her is a stupid mistake."

"Yeah," I growl, stepping closer and meeting his glare dead on. "Well, it's my fuckin' mistake, and I ain't givin' it up."

Then I turn and walk off, leavin' him standing in the dirt.

Fuck him.

Fuck Cade.

Fuck the lot of them.

PRESENT - CIARA

"Open the fuckin' door, Ciara!"

I blink, rubbing my eyes. What the *hell*? I glance at the clock on the wall above the television. It's about midnight. I fell asleep on the couch after my shift tonight; I didn't even make it to my bed. Now I have an angry biker at my door.

With a sigh, I slide off the couch and stand on wobbly legs. I walk to the front door and open it, to see a very angry Cade with one hell of a fat lip. His eyes are wild, and his expression tells me that I shouldn't open my mouth and say a word to him, or I'll risk getting my head torn clean off.

"Comin' in," he growls, shoving past me.

"How nice of you to visit me in the middle of the night," I mumble, running my fingers through my hair to untangle it.

"Couldn't find you, looked at the bar, they said you went home. So, I came here."

"And to what do I owe this delightful visit?"

He spins, glaring at me; I actually take a few steps back.

"You and Spike," he grates out. "That's what I'm fuckin' here for."

Uh-oh.

"What about us?" I say as casually as possible.

"Don't you fuckin' play with me! You're seein' him, and you didn't fuckin' tell me."

"It's got nothing to do with you," I point out.

He steps closer, anger rising to a level of no return. "Has everything to do with me. I told you he ain't right for you, that right now he ain't in a place to give you what you want, but you got stubborn and didn't fuckin' listen to me. He's bad news, Ciara. He ain't in a place to give you anything but a good fuck, and that's all you're gonna be, Tom Cat, a good time. You really want that? You really wanna be no more than a fuck?"

I want to slap him. I hate him right now. I hate him because he's right, and I know it. Right now, Spike doesn't want to give me anything more than a good time. I don't doubt there's lingering feelings between us, but I also know it's not enough to make him see me as anything more than what I am. Cade bringing it up only makes it hurt that much more. It hurts, because for me it goes so much deeper. For me, Spike is my soul. He's my reason to breathe. He's what I fight for.

"I love him," I yell, feeling my voice shake.

Cade's face drops and he sighs deeply, losing his anger. "Fuck, Tom Cat, when will you see he ain't ever gonna be what you need?"

"You don't know that," I whisper.

He steps forward, putting a hand on my shoulder and squeezing. "Do know that, 'cause I've known Spike longer than anyone. He's not going to break for anyone, or you..."

"How can you possibly know that?" I cry, walking over to the couch and dropping down. My legs are wobbly, and my body is shaking from the inside out.

"I told you, I know Spike and I know how fucked up he is. I was there, Ciara. I was in that car and I saw what it did to him. He ain't ever gonna move on from Chey's death, and he ain't ever gonna be normal again. You need to find yourself a man to fuckin' love you, not to just fuck you."

Hot tears fill my eyes, and instead of breaking, I get angry. I'm sick of being second best. Sick of everyone telling me I'll never compare. I'll never be *her*! Fuck her! Fuck her and the rest of them. I look up at Cade, and the tears slide down my cheeks.

"Leave, now."

His eyes widen a little. "Tom Cat, don't go kickin' me out 'cause of what I said. Only tryin' to look out for you."

"I said *leave*!" I hiss, my voice full of venom.

He flinches. "All right. Ain't gonna argue with a hurt woman."

I look away as he walks toward the door. When he gets to it, he turns to me and stares for what seems like forever.

"You know I'm right, Tom Cat. That's why it hurts so much. When you're ready to talk to me, you call yeah?"

Then he's gone.

I get off the couch, swiping angrily at my tears. I walk into the kitchen, open the cupboard, and pull out a full bottle of vodka. I pop the top, and bring it to my lips. The liquid burns so much I choke as it slides down my throat, but I don't care, I keep drinking. I'm tired of pain. I'm tired of the inner fight to be something different, but

140

most of all, I'm tired of always being Cheyenne's shadow. Even though she's gone, I still live behind her. Everything that she left behind affects me: Spike, my parents, my entire life…all broken because of her. I lean against the counter, heaving and coughing as I struggle to swallow more vodka. I want the pain gone, just for a fucking minute.

It goes away.

I find myself going through old photos, cursing and giggling all at the same time. I have a severe case of neglected child syndrome, if that's even a real thing.

I was always the child behind the star - Cheyenne being the star, *of course.* She was perfect, happy, witty, smart, and everything I wasn't. People noticed her, and if they didn't, she made sure they did. More often than not, I lived with it; until she took the one thing I loved the most - Danny.

I come across the picture of the three of us, just before Spike slept with me. It was a party; I think it was the first party where they officially got together. I remember how much it hurt. God, it fucking hurt. Nothing in the world feels worse than loving someone who doesn't love you back.

"Ciara!"

I flinch, and lift my hazy eyes to the front door. Spike. I don't move, partly because I'm so drunk and I can't. I don't drink often, and it's really not pretty when I do.

"You in there?" he yells again.

Yes, I'm in here. I'm not going to answer though.

"Fuckin' hell, open up. I can hear the fuckin' music."

I still don't move.

I hear him shuffling about, then I hear his boots crunching as he moves around to the window. Soon, it's being lifted and he's climbing in. I burst out into a fit of giggles, even though it's really not funny. Someone just climbed through my window, with little to no effort. *That's safe.*

Spike spins when he's on his feet and stares down at me on the floor, clutching my bottle of vodka. He has a busted eye, and he looks like shit, but his eyes soften a touch when he sees what I'm doing—or maybe I just think they do because I'm so drunk. He walks over, his eyes scanning over the photo album in my lap.

"What're you doin', Tom Cat?"

"I had a visitor today," I slur, sloshing my bottle around as I lift it.

"Give me that bottle," he says, kneeling down in front of me.

I note how good he looks this evening. He's wearing his leather jacket; fuck, I love that jacket. I love how it looks stretched across his broad back. He's wearing a navy blue t-shirt underneath it, and I just bet it's clinging to his hard body. His black jeans are old and ripped, and he has silver chains hanging off them. Fuck him for being so attractive. When he reaches for my bottle, I jerk it away.

"Ah-ah, mine."

"You're fuckin' smashed. Give me the bottle."

"You didn't let me finish." I wave, and the bottle sloshes about. "Cade came to visit me."

Spike grinds his jaw. "Give me the fuckin' bottle."

142

"Make me," I giggle.

He lunges forward, gripping the bottle with one hand and the back of my head with the other. I realize when my back hits the floor; he gripped the back of my head to stop it slamming down. His hard body lands on top of mine, and with a grunt, he tries to prop himself up. He manages to get the bottle standing upright beside us, before turning and glaring down at me.

"You fuckin' finished?"

"Yeah," I growl sarcastically. "I'm fuckin' finished."

"Smart mouthin' me ain't gonna save you, Ciara."

I snort. "What will save me, biker?"

"Tellin' me why the fuck you're drunk as twenty men, yellin' at photos of your sister."

"Your wife, you mean?"

He flinches, and his face flashes with hurt and rage. "Enough."

"Why?" I growl, getting in his face. "Why should I stop going on and on about princess Cheyenne?"

"You're walkin' a fine line, Ciara. Ain't a good idea to talk about my dead wife to me right now, and it sure as shit ain't a good idea to be smart mouthin' me when I'm already fuckin' pissed off."

"I couldn't care less how pissed off you are," I snap. "You're only here to fuck me, right?"

He doesn't say anything for a while, and just as I think he's about to, he lifts himself off me. He gets to his feet, leans down and hurls me up.

143

"Go and have a shower."

"No," I growl.

"You're fuckin' drunk, angry, and you need to shower and sleep."

"Don't tell me what I need!" I yell, shoving at his chest. "You don't care what I need."

"Ain't discussing this with a drunken, rambling girl!"

"You wouldn't discuss it with me anyway. You've already given me the lowdown! You'll fuck me, keep me around, you won't share me, but you'll never fucking give yourself to me, either. I'm no more than an easy fuck you can keep around. Why bother, Spike? Why don't you just walk away and never speak to me again?"

"I fuckin' tried!" he yells, stepping close. "I fuckin' tried, but you insisted on huntin' me down and tryin' to make it better. You wanted my forgiveness so you could move on and be happy again. You were the one who wanted to fuckin' fix somethin' that couldn't be fixed!"

"Then why are you here?" I cry, stumbling backwards. "Why bother?"

"We're not doin' this now, Ciara," he growls, his voice low and deep.

"Yes," I yell. "We are. You won't speak to me about this, you just keep shoving me away."

"Nothin' to fuckin' talk about!" he hisses. "Past is the fuckin' past."

"Then leave, Spike. I'm done talking to you, and I'm sure as shit done trying to help someone who refuses to let me in."

"Why do you fuckin' think that is?" he barks.

I cross my arms, and glare at him. "Oh, now you're going to talk!"

"You fuckin' stood in that courtroom, and you fuckin' brought me down with every scathing word. Then you wondered why I fuckin' hated you—and fuck, Ciara, I did fuckin' hate you."

Ouch. That hurts. It hurts far more than I ever imagined it would. I reel back, and my hand presses to my heart. I struggle to fight with the pain inside me, and I struggle to push it aside to let the anger I know is there through. When it finally shows its face, it's lethal, mean, and no doubt completely uncalled for.

"She was my fucking sister," I screech. "She had her fucking brains blown out while she was driving *YOU* to safety. I hated you for that, and I had every right to."

He jerks and his eyes flare. "You fuckin' bitch," he bellows. "You have no fuckin' idea! I never wanted her in that fuckin' car. *NEVER*. I wanted that fuckin' bullet, and I've wanted it every day since. You didn't stand in that courtroom to defend *her*, you did it to get back to me."

I lunge forward, and I hit him so hard in the jaw that his head spins to the side. He growls, gripping my hands and shoving me up against the wall. My head spins, and I struggle to gather my bearings. We're both panting, both having gone far and beyond normal retaliation. This is it. The moment we've needed to have for so many years now.

"I did hate her," I scream, shaking. "I did, because she took you. I loved you, and she took you. She went out of her way to take what was mine, and then she rubbed it in my face every fucking day after it.

"Then you fucked me, and god, I thought there was a chance. There was never a chance. Then she died, and I was so angry. I was so angry that you had put her in that position. I was angry at you for even involving yourself in her life, and I was angry that she left behind something so fucking beautiful, broken. She left you broken. She left me broken. And I've paid for it ever since.

"I went into that courtroom so ready to make you pay for all the pain left in my life. I never fucking said it was the right thing to do, and I tried to say sorry…"

"The damage was already done," he growls, his face so close to mine I can smell him and oh, he smells amazing. "You came back, and you fuckin' broke me. I was grieving, and you took Cade's side. You took his fuckin' side because of your anger toward me. You fuckin' ripped my heart out, and then you fuckin' stomped on it before shoving it back in my chest and expecting me to be okay with it. I'm not fuckin' okay with it!"

"I made a mistake," I throw back. "You, of all people, should understand that. You made a mistake too."

"Yeah," he barks. "And no fucker has forgiven me for it, so don't you fuckin' stand here wantin' something that nobody was willin' to give me when I needed it. You ain't gettin' my fuckin' forgiveness, Ciara, because I don't fuckin' have yours."

He pushes off the wall and turns, storming toward the open bottle of vodka. He grips it off the floor and brings it to his mouth, drinking in long, deep pulls until a good quarter of the bottle is gone.

"I do forgive you," I say, my voice small and weak.

He spins around and meets my gaze, and my heart begins to thud.

"You forgive me for Cheyenne, but you don't forgive me for puttin' my cock inside you and takin' your innocence."

I flinch and he snorts. "Yeah, exactly."

"You haven't given me a chance to forgive you, because all you've done is push me away. Every time I've tried to get close, you shove me back."

"He's a useless, pathetic biker. He put her in that car. He put her in that position. He's the reason she's dead. He should pay, every day of his life for it."

I jerk violently as he repeats the very words I said the day I stood up in court. Tears burn under my eyelids, and begin streaming down my face. My lip trembles, but I still manage to spit out my next words.

"I fucked up," I rasp. "I can't take those words back. I didn't mean them; you know I didn't mean them. I have fought to make that up to you, for years I have fought."

"You nearly put me away. If it wasn't for my fuckin' connections, I'd be in jail."

"I know that! I can't keep telling you I'm sorry. I can't live forever trying to make you see that I fucked up, that you were the best thing in my life and I let you walk away."

His body stiffens, and he begins breathing heavily again. "I heard you, the night of that party all those years ago. I fuckin' heard you tell Cheyenne she could have me."

"I know you did," I whisper.

"I was fuckin' gutted. You know, as hot as your sister was, I never had any fuckin' intention of bein' with her. I wanted one thing, and that was you. I tried, I showed it to you all the fuckin' time and you couldn't see it. Then that night, you basically shoved me toward her, and I realized you didn't want me. I was waiting for nothin', so I went with her. I fell in love with her, I was happy with her, but she was never fuckin' you, Ciara. Not even close."

"Why didn't you tell me? All those years, and you didn't say anything."

His eyes flare, and then soften. "Same goes, Ciara. Why didn't you tell me?"

I swallow. He's right. We were both idiots.

"We had a great friendship. I was scared if you didn't feel the same that I would ruin it."

He grunts, shaking his head slowly. "Yeah, well, same here."

I rub my arms. They're tingling, and my body feels like it might explode with emotion. "I made a mistake, Spike. The day I stood in that courtroom, I made a mistake. I'm sorry," I pause to take a deep, steady breath. "I know you can't forgive me, but I'm sorry all the same."

His eyes soften completely, and for a long moment we just stare at each other. "I'm sorry too, for fuckin' you the way I did. Never did it right, and I should have. I should have laid you down and made you feel as beautiful as I know you fuckin' are. You deserved better than what I gave you."

My lip trembles again, and his gaze softens even more. A glimpse of my Danny shows in his face, and I know we've finally cracked through the wall that has built up so thick between us.

"I don't want to hate you anymore, I don't want to fight anymore, I don't want any of this between us anymore…" I whisper.

"Yeah," he rasps. "Me either."

"Can we move on?"

He moves forward until he reaches me. He grips my face and leans down, pressing his lips softly against mine. "Yeah, Tom Cat, we can."

"What is it exactly we're doing here?" I dare to ask as he moves his lips down my neck.

"We're lettin' life take us where life is gonna take us, and this time, we're not gonna fuckin' fight it."

That sounds fine by me.

Just perfect.

CHAPTER 11

PAST - CIARA

"She's gone, Ciara, and she's never coming back. It doesn't matter what you want right now!" my mother yells, her eyes puffy from crying.

My sister has been gone for six weeks, and we've been through hell and back, fighting to get Danny put away. My heart has been ripped out, stomped on, rolled in the dirt, and ground into a thousand pieces during the last few months, and now my parents are refusing to acknowledge my life. They're grieving, I get that, but they aren't even trying to let me move on and find my own life. I wanted help with college, but they are refusing to give me money, blaming me entirely for Cheyenne's death. It's my fault that she's gone, because I was the one who befriended Danny. I ran away, instead of fighting to keep them apart like I should have.

"I can't keep living like this, Mom. I need a life. I need to get into school and try to create something that resembles some kind of normality."

"Cheyenne is dead!" she cries. "Dead, because of you and that idiot biker. Now I have to live without her. I can never hold her babies. That was my grandchild inside of her, and now he or she is dead, too. I don't care about your studies, Ciara. You have the chance to do whatever you want, Cheyenne doesn't. So go and do it!"

It hurts when your own mother has lost her love for you. It hurts because it's something that can't be changed. I was always second to Cheyenne, but now it's just like I'm in her way.

My father doesn't speak to me. He just lives in his office. I'm tired of feeling like this all the time. They hate me, and they aren't going to help me get to where I need to go. This one, I'm going to have to do on my own. I turn to my mother, and meet her puffy gaze. She sniffles, and swipes her fingers under her nose.

"I'm tired of this. It's clear to me you couldn't care less about what happens to me, so I'm going to leave. I'll go and find my own way, because I'm tired of living in Cheyenne's shadow, when she's not even alive."

My mother stands and slaps me so hard I see stars. I grip my cheek, fighting back the hurt and anger.

"How dare you? You always were jealous of her! I can't believe you would speak about her like that. She loved you, and this is how you honor her memory?"

"She loved herself!" I scream. "She didn't love me, and neither do you."

"Don't be so stupid. I do love you, but I'm not going to coddle you and make you feel better about something that is your doing."

"How is it my doing?" I cry, trembling. "She threw herself at Danny, it was her choice!"

"I don't believe that for a second! Not a second! She fell in love with a lie, and got herself trapped. She wanted out. She didn't want to be there. She told me so. She just couldn't leave because he got her pregnant."

"You are so naive!" I screech. "She wanted to be there. She wanted his body over hers, every night. She wanted his baby. She wanted him!"

"You shut your mouth," she hisses. "That is your sister you're talking about."

"And she's dead!" I scream so loudly I scare myself. "She's dead, and she's not coming back. It's not my fault. She was the one who opened her filthy legs for Danny, and she was the one who made sure he married her. She made her own choices!"

She slaps me again. Now tears are thundering down her cheeks. "You always were so selfish, Ciara. Get out of my house."

"Gladly," I spit.

I turn on my heel, and with shaky legs I walk to my room. I pack what little things I own, and ring a cab. As I'm walking down the hall, I stop at Cheyenne's door and peer into her old room. My heart hurts for my sister, because she didn't deserved to die. I'll always love her deep down in my soul, but I can't help that I will always hate her, too. She knew what she was doing, every step of the way, and she made a point of shoving my face in it. Now she's gone, and no one wants to hear of it. My parents hate me. Danny hates me. My world has turned upside down, and for what? For befriending someone who changed everyone's lives. I peer around the room one last time, and before I leave, I whisper one, simple sentence and I mean it. Oh, I mean it.

"Fuck you, Cheyenne."

~*~*~*~*~

PRESENT - CIARA

I giggle and twirl, letting my hair flow around me. Spike is sitting on my bed, watching me with an amused expression. I'm still tipsy, and having a great time. Spike has been drinking with me for

152

the last hour and we've both stop caring about anything else but this moment.

"You need to stop drinkin', yeah?" Spike grins.

"Later, babe."

He chuckles. "Since when do you call me babe?"

"Since now."

He wraps his fingers around the top of the bottle, and begins a gentle stroking, running his finger around the tip. I lick my lips and stop dancing, suddenly getting the urge to forget the drinking and make use of the hot biker sitting in front of me fucking my bottle with his fingers. God, I want those fingers inside me, deep and hard. I shudder, and Spike's gaze grows lazy.

"Somethin' you wanna say, baby?"

I drop to my knees, and begin crawling toward him, full of determination. I stop in front of him, lifting my hands and placing them on his jean clad legs. I shove gently, spreading his thighs until I can shuffle between them. He makes a growling sound and looks down at me, his dark eyes hooded.

"What're you doin', Tom Cat?"

"Something I've so desperately wanted to do…" I husk, gripping his belt and unbuckling it.

"Baby, don't wanna just fuck you and make you think that's all I'm here for…"

"But Spike," I purr, looking up at him. "I wanna be fucked."

"Fuck, Ciara," he rasps. "You're makin' my cock hard."

Oh God. My pussy clenches so hard I have to rub my thighs together to stop myself from exploding with need. Spike reaches down, gripping either side of my face with his big, heavy hands. I peer up at him, still running my fingers over the buckle of his belt.

"Tell me what it is you want to do…"

I lick my lips, and look him dead in the eye. "I want to take your spikes out."

His chest rumbles, and he reaches around, running his thumb over my bottom lip. "Fuck yeah, Tom Cat."

"I've always wanted to…tell me how…"

"Baby," he hisses through clenched teeth. "Just use them fuckin' pretty lips, and own it."

I'll own it all right - I'll *nail* it. I tug at his jeans, popping the top button. He moves his hips, and allows me to pull them down his legs. I grip his boots when I reach them, and pull them off before removing his jeans completely.

When I look back up, I see he's not wearing anything else under his jeans. From this angle, I can see every piercing in his cock. I let my eyes linger over the line of them running up the inside of his length. Each one has a tiny spike on the end, but when he's hard and pulsing like this…it just looks, well, dangerous. The one right though the head has bigger spikes, and God, I want to run my tongue all over it.

I raise myself up, wrapping my hand around his cock and gently squeezing. He hisses and cups my face, gripping me with just enough pressure to turn me on. I lean down, swiping my tongue over the large spike in the tip. Spike groans, deep and throaty, as I work my tongue around it, tracing the sharp tip and teasing him until he's

154

panting above me. Then I close my teeth over it, and nip it. It pops off, leaving just the rounded end of the barbell. I drop the spike into my hand, and continue working my tongue down his length, biting and tugging, pulling and jerking until he's growling so loudly his body trembles. When I reach the last of the spikes, I nip it off and drop it into my hand, before lowering my mouth and sliding my tongue out and over his balls.

"Fuck, Ciara, baby…I wanna come."

Hearing him pretty much beg makes me want to tease him even more. So, I do. I run my tongue over his balls, up and down his cock, and over his head until he's growling and tangling his fists in my hair, tugging my mouth toward him. Before I know what's happening, he leans down and scoops me up. In ten seconds flat, my back is pressed against the wall and he's crushed against me. I reach out, dropping the spikes on the table beside me, before reaching up and tangling my fingers into his hair, bringing his lips down over mine. God, he tastes so fucking divine. Like Spike mixed with the warm, but intense flavor of vodka. Our tongues slide together, and his cock presses hard against my belly.

"Goin' to fuck you now baby, hard…fuckin' hard. You ready?"

"Yes," I rasp against his lips. "Fuck, yes."

He grips my shorts, jerking them down angrily. I shuffle out of them, kicking them to the side. He grips my panties, tearing them off. I giggle and bite his earlobe, which earns me a growl so sexy I find it hard to hold myself back. Spike reaches around, gripping my ass and pulling me to him, forcing me to grind against his erection. Oh god, the feeling of that hard length pressing up and down against my slick heat…it's incredible.

"Think I can make you come like this, baby?"

155

"Yes," I hoarsely whisper. "God, Spike…"

"What do you fuckin' call me in here?"

"Danny," I cry out as he rubs and rubs, sliding that perfect piercing over my clit.

"Yeah," he growls. "Fuck, yeah."

I come, and it's so powerful I take skin off the shoulder I'm clenching onto. He gives me a deep, throaty growl, and I give him one deep, intense scream as I convulse without him even putting his cock inside me.

I'm still rattling from my orgasm when he grips my leg, bringing it up and around his hip. Then he's pressing against me, fuck, he's right there…stretching, filling, making that orgasm drag out longer. He pushes inside me, *deep*. We both hiss at each other, like two feral cats. His hand is on my ass, using it to drive his thrusts. My fingers are in his hair, tugging harshly, pulling with desperate need. Our lips keep clashing, blending together in desperate, hungry kisses.

"So fuckin' sweet," Spike rasps in my ear. "Wanna stay buried in you forever."

I'm so close, my body is wound up so tight that I can feel every, deep, long thrust. I can feel myself tightening around him. God, I'm so close.

Spike reaches between us, and he flicks my clit. Literally, flicks it. The pain combined with the pleasure sends me over the edge and I scream, fuck do I scream. I come so hard my body shakes around him. He quickens his pace, and our skin slaps together, loudly. His cock swells inside me and I feel it beginning to pulse.

"Shit," he bellows, clutching my ass so hard I have no doubt he'll leave bruises.

He drags his cock in and out until he's wrung every, last drop from his body. I let my body relax, panting with pure relief. I drop my head onto his chest, inhaling the scent of him combined with the leather of his jacket. I'll never forget that smell. It's perfect.

He grips the back of my head, cupping me with his hand. We stay like that for a long moment, and I feel his nose in my hair, breathing me in. This moment, it's incredible. It's mind-blowing. It's *real*. It's quite possibly the most real moment we've ever had.

"Gotta shower now, babe."

"Yeah," I mumble.

He reaches down, gripping my other leg and lifting me so I'm straddling him. Then he carries me toward the bathroom.

I nestle my nose into his neck and just breathe. We reach the shower, and he puts me down. Sulking, I pout at him. He flashes me a super grin, then begins taking his clothes off...well...only the top half, considering he isn't wearing pants.

I watch with a lazy smile as he slides his shirt up and over his head. I stare at his massive, tattooed body and sigh. I could look at him forever, and never get bored. He's just so beautiful. I grip the last of my clothes, dragging them over my head until we're both standing in front of each other, fully naked.

I turn, stepping into the shower, and turning it on. The warm water sprays over my body, and I groan. Spike steps in behind me and wraps his arms around my middle, pressing his hard chest against my back. I groan, dropping my head back into his chest and just standing there, enjoying every second.

He runs his fingers up and down my belly, and I reach down, tangling mine in his. He lets me hold his hand for a while, before he lets go and reaches down, gripping the soap, and pumping some into his hand. He rubs it over my body, causing little whimpers to escape me. He finds my ass, and grips it again, spinning me and pulling me toward him.

"You're an ass man," I murmur into his chest.

"Babe, I fuckin' love your ass."

"Oh?"

"Always have."

"Really?" I say, licking his nipple.

He shudders and grips my hair, tugging my head back so I'm looking up at him. "Stop lickin' my nipple, my cock is gettin' hard again."

"Maybe I want it to," I grin, grinding myself against him.

"When did you get so…adventurous?"

"When I lost the man I loved because I wasn't adventurous enough…"

His eyes fill with guilt, and a little anger. "Yeah, well, past is past."

"Yeah, but the past defines who we are in the future…"

He grins. "So smart."

"I can't help it, it's the good breeding."

He snorts, and I narrow my eyes.

"What?" I say, stepping back. "Are you saying I don't have good breeding?"

"Babe," he says, stepping closer and pulling me back to him. "I know you've got good fuckin' breeding. I also know that you're the only one that got the brains."

"Cheyenne was smart..." I dare to say.

"Cheyenne used her looks to get what she wanted, don't take brains to do that."

"Yeah," I say, quietly. "I guess."

"No more talkin' about that shit, ain't no point."

I swallow and nod. Part of me will always be jealous that my sister got him first; how can I not be? What I just experienced then, she probably experienced many times over. The thought puts a crushing pain in my heart, and I struggle to keep my breath steady. I'm jealous of my dead sister, and I don't know if I can ever take that away. She had what I wanted, and the only reason I have it now is because she's gone. If she didn't die...

"Fuckin' stop it," Spike growls.

I look up at him. "What?"

"Thinkin'. I can see it, babe. I know what you're thinkin'."

"No," I whisper. "You don't."

"You're thinkin' that I've been here with Cheyenne before. You're thinkin' that I fucked her the way I just fucked you. You're thinkin' you're always goin' to be second..."

I flinch, answering him without even opening my mouth. He snorts. "Let me tell you somethin', and listen close 'cause I will *not*

159

be fuckin' sayin' this to you every fuckin' day. If you can't deal with my past, and what went down, then you walk away.

"As for Cheyenne, what I had with her was very different. Cheyenne didn't fuck, she made love. Cheyenne didn't share a shower, 'cause she liked her own space and was in love with herself. There ain't no comparison, and there never will be. I'm not sayin' I didn't love her. She was my wife, she was growin' my baby, I fuckin' loved her, but the emotion I feel with you was never there with her. You make my fuckin' heart hurt. You make my body so fuckin' wound up with need it aches. You make my fuckin' days bright, and not one of those fuckin' days has passed that you haven't been in my head. Might have had her first, might have fuckin' loved her first, but you're the one who ends this with me."

Fuck. Crap. Shit.

I hate when he says things like that, because it makes me feel childish...and maybe that's what I'm being, childish.

"Not goin' to live the rest of my life tryin' to tell you that what I felt for your sister is different. Not goin' to tell you every day that you and she don't even compare, because you're two different people. Not goin' to keep assuring you that you're not second to me, that in fact, you were fuckin' first. You wanna be in this with me, Tom Cat, or you don't."

"I do," I whisper.

"Then we ain't gonna talk about this anymore."

I nod, swallowing.

"We're goin' to get out, get into your bed, and I'm gonna fuck you real slow. Then we're goin' to lie next to each other. I don't cuddle, but I will rub your hair until you're asleep."

160

Shit.

How can something so blunt sound so fucking sweet?

"Okay."

"Okay babe."

We get out of the shower, and he does just that. He fucks me real slow, bringing me to orgasm twice more, then he lays beside me, ringed fingers in my hair, stroking until I'm asleep.

CHAPTER 12

PAST - SPIKE

"Stop worrying about her," Cheyenne snaps, rubbing her fingers over her slightly swelling belly.

"She's your fuckin' sister, sunshine, she deserves to know."

"She doesn't answer the phone, she doesn't want a part in this."

"Don't matter. She still deserves to know."

"Why are you always on her side, Spike? I know you two were friends and all that bullshit, but honestly, sometimes I think you wish you picked her!"

I sigh. Here we fuckin' go again. I love my wife, fuckin' adore her, but fuck…she gets something in her head and she don't let it go. On and on, around and around, we go on about Ciara and my friendship with her.

I've been tryin' for motherfuckin' years to get in contact with her and attempt to make things better, but she won't hear it. My fault, really. I fucked her and treated her like shit. She thinks it was to get back at Cheyenne, and part of it was, but shit…most part was 'cause I wanted inside that girl from the day she turned eighteen and it was the best fuckin' night of my life. Cheyenne will never know that, though. No, she'd flip her fuckin' lid.

"Enough of that shit, Cheyenne. We've talked about it, and I told you to fuckin' stop bringin' it up. I'm only thinkin' of you and your relationship with her."

"Yeah, one that she refuses to have because she doesn't like that you picked me."

I sigh again. "Don't fuckin' matter why, I think you need to tell her."

"You know she hasn't called Momma for months?"

Can't say I blame her. Their mother is a cunt. Yep, a cunt.

"Your Momma treats her like a dog."

Cheyenne crosses her arms. "She does not."

"Babe, I'm done talkin' about this. I'm sick of it and it's startin' to piss me off. If you want to keep goin' on about it, I'm leavin' to go and see the boys."

Seeing that she's not going to get any further with me, her eyes soften and she steps forward. "You know I love you, and I love Ciara, but this is my moment…I want to enjoy it. It's not always about her."

No, it's never about her, that's the fuckin' problem.

"Yeah babe, whatever you want."

"I love you, Spike…you know that…"

"I know."

"And you love me?"

"Forever sunshine…"

And forever is a fuckin' long time.

~*~*~*~

PAST - CIARA

"She was a virgin, you piece of shit!"

I can hear my sister screaming at Danny downstairs, but I can't bring myself to move. Tears stream down my face, the reality of the situation crushing my soul. Danny had sex with me last night, and for a while, I thought it was because he wanted to. Turns out, it was all for Cheyenne's benefit. She went off on one of her little fits, and decided to use another man to make him jealous. Angry, he came to find me, and one thing led to another. I didn't tell him it was my first time. I came home, sobbing because I figured it out, and my sister found me. She asked me what happened, I told her, and everything came to light. She was jealous and angry, and I was downright heartbroken.

"I didn't fuckin' know!"

"How could you?! How could you fuck her, Spike?"

"Thought you were movin' on. I was sick of playin your fuckin' games."

"So you fucked my sister to get back at me?"

That hurts, God, it hurts. I heave and my eyes burn from the salty tears continually leaking out of them. I wrap my arms around my mid-section and I cry and cry. *A revenge fuck.* That's what I was. A fucking revenge fuck! I was no more than a way to get back at Cheyenne.

He broke me. He truly tore me apart. My body is aching, a reminder of what went on last night. I'm trying not to think about it,

164

but the images are haunting me. The way he touched me, the way he ran his fingers over my body…god…he made it feel so real. I *thought* it was real.

"God, you taste so fucking good," he growls, swirling his tongue around my clit.

I arch my back, gripping the sheets and whimpering his name. Over and over, his tongue swirls around my swollen nub, bringing me to orgasm embarrassingly fast. His fingers are deep inside me, pressing, causing me to become wet around him. His lips have been all over my body. Every part of me is now his.

I will never forget the moment he moves up my body. His eyes are on mine, and oh, I'm desperate to kiss him. He hasn't kissed me, I don't know why, and I don't care. He's here. He's with me, and that's all that matters. I watch with hooded eyes as he rolls on a condom. He removed the spikes; he must have taken them out before he came here, because I can't see them and I've heard from enough sources that they're there.

His body moves over mine, and he puts his lips to my shoulder, soothing me before he presses inside. A stab of pain travels through my body, and I take hold of him, whimpering. He pushes in further, growling loudly and tangling his fingers in my hair. I cry out, but it sounds so similar to a cry of pleasure that Danny doesn't notice it's that of pain, too. He sheaths himself, and then gently pulls back out.

"You're so tight, baby, so tight."

I shudder, and wrap myself around him, tilting my hips to meet each of his deep, intense thrusts. The pain eventually eases and is replaced by pleasure so powerful, my mind spins. I close my eyes, arching my back and whimpering his name as he moves. His growls combine with my whimpers, and we make a magical sound all of our own. I have imagined this many times over, but this, this is so much better than I could have ever dreamed up.

"She's devastated!" Cheyenne screams, snapping me out of my moment.

"Then let me speak to her, and tell her I fucked up."

"No, you're going to stay away from her. She doesn't want you, Spike…she is so angry at you right now. If you care about her at all, you'll leave her alone."

"Didn't wanna fuckin' hurt her!"

"Well you did, and you hurt me, too."

"I fucked up," he barks. "So did you."

"I didn't fuck someone else!"

"Fuck, Cheyenne…"

I cover my ears, getting to my feet. My body hurts, and my eyes burn. I reach under my bed and grip my suitcase. I toss my clothes and belongings into it, and I wipe my tears dry. I won't cry another tear for Danny. Not fucking one.

I can't do this anymore. It hurts too much, my heart can't handle another moment listening to them argue about me. Like I am just a huge mistake. I can't watch him choose her, and I can't sit around pretending like that wouldn't bother me. It does, and I won't live a second longer pretending it doesn't.

I can still hear them arguing outside so I take my things, and I head downstairs. They're out the back of the house, so they don't even notice that I'm moving around. They're too busy arguing. I stop at my parent's room on the way out and I take their savings in cash, then I take one last, long look at my house before heading out the front door. I get into my car, start it and, swallowing hard, I reverse it out of the driveway. No way in hell will I be anyone's revenge fuck, and I certainly won't live as second best.

I need to get out of here.

I just can't do it anymore.

CHAPTER 13

PRESENT - CIARA

I hear a bellow of pain, and I jerk awake. It takes me a moment to realize where I am, and what's happening. Spike is beside me, thrashing in the sheets. His body is covered in sweat and he's arching his back, gripping the sheets so hard his knuckles are white. He cries out again, tossing his head from side to side.

My heart begins to thump, and I feel awful for him. My stomach churns, because I know what he's dreaming about. I know what he sees in his head every time he closes his eyes. He sees Cheyenne, and he shouldn't have to see her. He's living with so much guilt, and it's slowly destroying him.

I gently reach over, touching his shoulder. "Spike, hey, it's ok."

He thrashes again, calling out her name. I swallow, and I can't help it when I begin to cry. God, the poor man. I put my hand on his shoulder once more, shaking a little harder to try and get him to wake up. I know it's risky; I'm touching a massive man who's having a nightmare. He could easily swing his fist my way and cause big problems for both of us.

I can't let him suffer any longer, though; he's in pain. I shake him again, and he groans, fluttering his eyes open. I can see the moisture in them, and fuck, it hurts my heart. It really hurts. I don't bother blinking my tears away.

"Hey, you're okay, it's okay."

He stares at the roof for a moment, and then he turns his face to me. I can see he's confused, but I can also see when reality dawns. He swallows, and his face…it's broken. He's broken.

God, what an idiot I've been. I never looked at the black and white of the situation. I can see it now, plain and simple. Spike is fucking broken because he witnessed his own wife being shot. That's it. Plain and simple.

Tears thunder down my cheeks, and I reach across, gripping his face and running my thumb over the one tear that slides down his cheek. For a man like Spike, that might as well be him crying a waterfall.

"Baby," I rasp. "I'm so sorry. I'm so sorry you lost her."

He heaves, and turns his face away from me. His body shakes so violently, it worries me, but I let him go. He needs to feel this. He needs to just *feel*. I place my fingers on his chest, and I can feel his heart hammering under them.

"I'm so sorry, Danny. So sorry I didn't just see this for what it was. I thought of myself, and I didn't think enough of you. You lost your wife and your baby. God, I'm so sorry for that."

He makes a pained sound and sits up, swinging his legs over the side of the bed. He puts his head in his hands and his body starts shaking even harder. I put my hand on his back, and I scoot closer. He turns to the side, looking at me, cheeks wet with pain that runs so deep, even I could never imagine it.

I take his head, and I bring it down to my chest and he turns, wrapping his arms around my tiny body, and holding me so tightly I can hardly breathe. I let him. With my arms around his head, I hold him against my heart, letting him get it all out. If that takes all night, I'll sit here all night.

"Shhh, baby, it's okay."

He doesn't say anything, he just sits there, holding onto me like he never wants to let me go. My legs begin to ache, and his body grows heavier, but I don't complain. He needs this.

All along, he's just needed someone. He never had anyone to break to. His best friend was gone, his wife was dead, and he had no family. God, I was such a fucking bitch. I'm a terrible person.

I stroke his thick hair, swallowing back my tears. How selfish I was. I feel him begin to move, and I look down as he lifts his head and looks up at me. He reaches up, gripping my face. I let him. He brings his lips up to mine. I let him. He moves us, so his body is over mine and my back is on the bed. I let him.

Then his lips are on mine, soft, gentle, and sweet as hell. His hands are in my hair, stroking, gently soothing me, even though it's him who needs to be soothed. I close my eyes, and tears slip heavily down my cheeks. He wipes them away, and he deepens his kiss. I spread my legs, letting him shift between them, and I gently place them on either side of his body. He pushes inside me, his cock hard and full, stretching me. He begins to move, slow, beautiful. More tears fall, because I realize what he's doing.

He's making love to me.

I reach up, running my fingers up and down his sweat slicked back. He rocks his hips, gently, beautifully, bringing me to the edge. I bury my face in his neck, and I breathe him in, not wanting this moment to end.

Not a sound passes between us, and that's perfectly ok. We don't need to say anything. There are no words that could ever describe what we're both feeling right now.

Instead, he's showing me. He's showing me with his lips. He's showing me with his body. He's showing me with his heart. He

170

rocks in and out of my body until I'm silently shuddering around him, my orgasm warming me from the inside out. He follows a moment later, burying his head into my shoulder and pulsing deep inside me.

Then we just lay there, both of us breathing heavily. I run my fingers up and down his back, tickling his skin softly. For a long while, he doesn't move, but finally he rolls off me. He hooks one arm around my body, and takes me with him, making sure I land in the crook of his arm. I rest my head there, and we just lie in pure silence, neither of us wanting to speak—or perhaps we just don't know what to say. How do you speak in a situation like this? He knows how I feel, I know how he feels, now we're just leaning on each other, hoping that maybe, just maybe, the other person might take a touch of the pain away.

"She wanted to get in the car," he rasps.

I blink, and then I realize what's happening. He's telling me what happened…he's opening up. I stroke his abs, letting him know I'm listening.

"She didn't ask questions, she just got in the car. She kept it cool, takin' charge.

"She was fine, until she saw the bikes. She was okay, and then they showed up and she started to panic. Fuck, she was so scared. I'll never forget how scared she was in that last moment."

I heave, because I have never stopped to think about the moments before Cheyenne's death, and how scared she must have been. I break. I start to cry so much that I can't breathe.

I struggle out of Spike's arms, and roll off the bed. He sits up, his eyes wide and confused as I stumble toward the bathroom. I reach the toilet, drop to my knees, and I throw up. I heave and heave,

171

my body shaking with pain, and loss. I finally break down. I hated my sister for what she did. I hated that she was the golden child. I hated the life we had, but fuck, I loved her so much. I didn't realize how much until right now, when Spike gave me an image of her terrified before she died.

I scream.

I scream and hit the sides of the bowl with my fists, and then I reach up and tangle my fingers in my hair. We never had a chance. Not a chance. We never had great parents, we were always treated differently and therefore we always treated each other badly. We were never encouraged to love each other. I was a bad sister, and she was amazing. If we had a chance, if our parents were normal, and our lives were different, we would have had the chance to just be sisters. To love each other. To fight for each other. To breathe for each other. To always have each other's backs. To never hurt each other.

"Cheyenne," I scream, pulling out strands of my hair. "Oh god, Cheyenne."

Spike wraps his arms around me from behind, and he pulls me backwards. We crash onto the floor, and I scream again. He grips my fingers, pulling them from my hair, forcing them down by my sides. Pinning them there, he holds me so tightly I can't move.

"Cheyenne," I bellow loudly. "I want her back. I want another chance. I want to be the sister I should have been. I want to defy my parents, and fight to show her we could have been so different. I want to fight and tell her not to touch you, and then she would have moved on and found someone else. God, I want her back."

The words are broken, desperate and pathetic. Spike rocks me, backwards and forwards, as I wail for the sister I lost.

172

"I love her, I wanted her to know that. She never knew that because all we did was fight. I was so angry at her. Even after she died, I was so fucking angry at her. I never just told her I loved her."

"She knew," Spike rasps.

"No," I sob.

"Yeah," he says, pressing his face against mine and rocking us both harder.

"I'm so sorry, Spike. I'm so sorry about Cheyenne. I'm so sorry about your baby. I'm so sorry I was never there. I'm so sorry I hurt you."

"Baby," he soothes, his voice broken. "I know."

"I want the pain to go away. It hurts," I whimper.

"I know."

He slows his rocking, and my tears gently begin to subside. When they finally stop, my eyes burn and my body hurts. It feels like I've run a marathon. Spike gently lets me go and he turns me around, running his finger over my puffy, red eyes.

"Fuck, Ciara, you're hurtin' me."

"I'm sorry," I croak.

"No, baby, don't you be sorry."

"I shouldn't have done that, it wasn't about me and—"

He puts a finger to my lips. "She was your sister longer than she was ever my wife. You had every right to do that."

I reach over and cup his face. "I love you, Spike. I don't expect you to love me back, and I'm not asking you to even try. I just want you to know, that after everything, I still love you. I always have, and I always will."

His jaw tightens, and he leans in close, bringing his lips over mine softly, slowly, deeply. When he pulls back our eyes meet, and so much passes between us.

"Yeah," he rasps. "Baby, I know."

I know he knows.

I've always known he knows.

I just wanted him to know again.

CHAPTER 14

PRESENT - CIARA

I wake before Spike in the morning, and I can't bring myself to disturb him. He's sleeping soundly, which I imagine is something he doesn't do often. His big hands are tucked up behind his head, and his bare chest is rising and falling with every deep breath.

I slide out of bed, and my body aches all over. It's funny, when you have a night where you release a mass amount of emotion, you always wake up the next day feeling like you've been hit by a bus. It's almost like every part of your body has been holding those emotions, unable to let go, and then suddenly they release in a rush that puts you into some sort of shock. I feel numb, and yet completely sore. It's odd.

I lean down and grab Spike's shirt, pulling it over my head and breathing in his musky scent. Then, I tiptoe out of the room, closing the door silently.

I walk down the hall, opening the shutters as I go. When I reach the kitchen, I flick on the coffee machine and realize it's past 9 a.m. Jesus. I slept in far more than I normally would. I reach up into the cupboard, getting myself a cup, and begin brewing a coffee.

I dig through the fridge while I wait, wondering what I can make for Spike. I've got some bacon and eggs. That will work. Men love protein. I've just pulled them out of the fridge, when someone knocks on my front door. I let out a groan; who could possibly want me right now?

I walk over to the door, and swing it open to see Cade and Addison. Dammit. Shit. Fuck. They are NOT going to be happy when they find out Spike is here.

Well, Addison will be happy, Cade won't be. I cross my arms over my chest and force a smile. "Hey guys, what's up?"

Cade rakes a gaze over me, and his eyes blaze. Shit.

"Hey," Addi grins. "Interrupting something?"

"No! I was just making coffee."

"Whose shirt is that?" Cade says, his voice icy.

"Um...."

I don't get to finish because Spike walks out of the hallway, butt naked. I squeal, and he leaps backwards. His eyes widen when he sees Addi and Cade, and he just stands there, looking stupid. Fuck.

I turn back to them, cheeks flushing, no words. Addi tilts her head to the side, and it takes me a moment to realize she's looking at the spikes, or trying to. Sweet god, the girl has no shame. Cade grips her shoulder harshly, and pulls her back. Spike backs down the hall, and we just stand there in silence.

Well. Shit. Cade is pissed, like mega pissed. His eyes are flaring, and his lips are stretched in a tight line. I open my mouth to speak, but nothing comes out. That's when Addi steps in, and being her typical smart-ass self, she begins singing, "H-h-h-h-he works out!"

I stare at her, wide-eyed as she sings it using the same tone as LMFAO's song "Sexy and I Know It." I can't help myself - I burst out laughing. She grins, joining in and before we know it, Cade is laughing, too.

Spike walks back out, a pair of jeans on, still no shirt. Oh, right, I'm wearing it. I stop laughing, and everyone else follows suit. Cade stares at Spike, and for a moment, they just kind of eye each other. I really hope we don't end up with any more black eyes, because seriously, it's not necessary.

I turn back to Cade, reaching out and touching his arm. He flinches and meets my gaze. I know I'm giving him a pleading look, but I want this to be okay.

"Cade, please, this is important to me. I want to be with him. I want to remain friends with you. I don't want to have to choose, please don't make me."

His eyes soften a touch. "I'm only tryin' to protect you, Ciara. I don't wanna see you gettin' hurt again."

"I won't," I whisper.

He lifts his eyes to meet Spike's again. "You serious about this?"

I turn, and see Spike's eyes are on me. He stares at me a long moment, then he turns back to Cade. "Yeah, fuckin' serious."

Cade nods. "Ain't my place to tell you who to love, but fuck, you hurt her and I'll…"

"Yeah," Spike grunts. "I know."

"Okay," I say, breathing out. "Can we all get along then?"

"Yeah," Cade mutters.

"Yeah," Spike grunts.

Addi rolls her eyes and walks inside. She passes Spike, and flashes him an award-winning smile. "Morning friend!"

"Precious," he says, his mouth twitching.

"Have you got any coffee?" she says, walking into my kitchen.

I give Cade another glance and then I turn, flashing Spike a grin and walking into the kitchen with Addi. I watch as Spike walks over to Cade, and they lean in close. I tilt my head to the side, trying to catch what Spike is saying, but I can't make it out. Addi grips my arm, pulling me back. I turn to face her, and smile at her gleeful expression.

"We're two lucky bitches," she breathes, watching the two men.

"Yeah," I agree. "We sure are."

"So." She grins, spinning towards me. "You and Spike, yeah? Finally!"

I roll my eyes at her. "It's not serious, we're just not fighting it anymore."

"Hubba hubba!"

I laugh and pull out the coffee I was brewing and hand her a cup. She takes it, still grinning.

"So, you have to tell me....the spikes?"

I flush, and pour myself a coffee. "The stories are all true."

"Oh god, did he make you take them out with your teeth?"

I giggle. "He didn't *make* me..."

"You are such a rebel!"

I shrug. "What can I say, he brings out the best in me!"

Cade and Spike pull apart, walking into the kitchen. Spike walks up behind me, wrapping his arms around my waist. I shudder, and lean into him. Mmmm, far out, he smells good in the morning. He leans down, and whispers into my ear, "Lookin' fine in my shirt, Tom Cat."

I grin, and meet Addi's joyful expression. "Aw, you two!"

Spike chuckles, and Cade rolls his eyes. "Sugar, you're too fuckin' soft."

"They're adorable!" she says, leaning back into Cade.

"You ladies up for a ride today?" Spike asks. "We got club business to sort in the city."

I feel my heart begin to thump. Spike is taking me on a ride? Oh hell YES! Addi grins, nodding her head enthusiastically.

"You know I love riding with the guys. Are your guys coming too, Spike?"

"Yeah," Spike answers. "Got some shit we both gotta sort. We'll go for a ride together."

I know that's odd, which tells me they're up to something. Now isn't the time to bring it up, though. I'm too excited about having the chance to get on the back of Spike's bike.

"I'm in," I say, sipping my coffee.

"Right, well, feed me, woman, and then we'll hit the road."

I drive my elbow back into his stomach, and he grunts. Cade laughs, no doubt loving seeing Spike receive a little pain.

"Make yourself some food!"

Spike wraps his arms tighter around me and leans down again. "Careful baby, I like it rough."

"You like it all kinds of ways, you kinkster!" Addi says.

Spike laughs, and I roll my eyes, again. I turn, releasing myself from Spike's arms to begin making us some breakfast.

"You guys hungry?" I ask Cade and Addi.

"Yeah," they both say as soon as I pull out the bacon.

Typical. Whenever bacon and eggs are involved, everyone is suddenly hungry.

Can't say I blame them.

~*~*~*~

We hit the road as soon as breakfast is finished and we've gotten changed. I climb onto the back of Spike's bike, and Addison gets on Cade's. We follow them back to the Hell's Knights compound, and the guys are all waiting on their bikes, there's about ten of them. They join the group and we proceed to the Heaven's Sinners warehouse. Spike's guys are ready, and they too join us. When we're all on the road, flying down the highway, Cade, Spike, Jackson and Granger leading, I feel my heart swell. It's an intense feeling to be in a group so powerful, so deadly, and so close. I grip Spike tighter, feeling a smile spread across my face. It just doesn't get any better than this.

We arrive in the city after a few hours, and my butt is completely numb by the time I get off Spike's bike. I rub it, groaning and pouting. Spike laughs, and I shoot him a look. "Don't even think about saying anything."

He flashes me a beautiful, lazy smile. "Need to paddle that ass a bit more, toughen it up."

"You paddle my ass, and I'll drop you on yours."

He throws his head back and laughs, and the sound is like music to my heart. I haven't heard him laugh like that since I've been back. I want to put my hand over my heart and burst into a fit of pathetic tears. Even his guys stop what they're doing and turn to stare at him as though they're looking at a ghost. When he stops laughing, he turns and stares at them all. "What?"

They all turn away, shaking their heads. I grip Spike's jacket, pulling him close and bringing my lips to his. When we pull apart, I whisper, "You look so hot when you laugh."

"Got a surprise for you after we're done here, Tom Cat."

"Oh?" I say huskily.

"Yeah, oh. I know you'll love it, 'cause you're just like me."

Just like him. Hmmmm.

"When do I get it?"

He leans down, pressing a hard kiss to my lips.

"Later, Tom Cat."

I drop my bottom lip and he smirks, leaning in to run his tongue over it. I grip his shirt, pulling him closer and pressing my body up against his.

"Will you two get a fuckin' room!" one of the guys yells out.

Spike throws the rude finger up, then grips hold of me and kisses me so deep and hard my legs begin to wobble. By the time he lets me go I'm panting, flushing and wanting to take him somewhere private and rip his clothes off. Dammit. He grins at me once more, then turns to the group. "Right, we're gonna keep ridin' from here. You ladies need to go and busy yourselves for a few hours. We'll come back when we're done."

There are only two other Old Ladies on the ride today, aside from Addison and I. Though, technically I'm not an Old Lady.

The other two ladies walk off toward town, not even giving Addison and I a glance. Well, fine. Addi skips over to me, hooking her arm through mine. "We are going shopping!"

I smile at her, excited at the thought. I haven't been shopping for a long time, and I'm quite excited at the thought of having a girl's day out. It's my only day off work this week, and I can't think of a better way to spend it. Well, besides having Spike deep inside me.

"You better be lookin' after my girl, precious," Spike says to Addi.

She waves her hand at him. "Yeah, yeah, we'll be fine."

He raises his brows at her, then moves those brown eyes toward me. "You good?"

I give him a half-smile. "Yeah, I've been shopping alone before…"

He gives me a 'That's not funny' expression, and then reaches into his pocket, pulling out his wallet. I have my hand up before he can even open it. "Don't even think about it, you sure as shit aren't giving me money."

He narrows his eyes. "Tom Cat…"

He has a warning tone, but I'm not having a bar of it. "No, I'm not taking it."

"You know I don't have time to argue…"

"Then don't." I grin, pulling Addi closer.

"Fine, but you need anything, you fuckin' call yeah?"

"Got ya!"

"You fuckin' behave, sugar," Cade calls to Addi.

She blows him a kiss and then we both spin, walking off toward the stores. I'm nearly bouncing with excitement. It's been a long time since I've been shopping, let alone shopping with a friend.

Addi and I duck into the first shop we find, and pull out a range of dresses and shoes to try on. For the next hour we laugh and twirl, really not that interested in buying the dresses, but having a hell of a time putting them on. We pick out the prettiest shoes and the nicest hats, and we dance around the change rooms. Addi is quickly becoming my best friend, and I'm so glad to have finally found someone I understand.

When we're done with shopping, we head to a local café. After ordering some drinks, we get chatting about the guys and the club. She tells me how things with her and Cade are going, and how she and Jackson are becoming really close. She tells me about the Old Ladies treating her differently because she's Jack's little girl, and how much it pisses her off.

I tell her about Spike and me, and how we've finally broken the ice. We laugh, we get serious, and we have a fantastic time.

After lunch, and then head down to the beach and sit on the sand, rubbing our toes in it, and staring out at the ocean. I wonder, while we're sitting there, if she knows anything that's going down between the clubs.

"Do you know what they're up to?" I ask.

She turns to me, pulling her sunglasses down over her eyes. "Who?"

"The clubs."

She shakes her head. "No, they don't discuss it with us. I've picked up a few things from hearing Cade on the phone, though."

"And…" I prompt.

"Ciara, I love you honey, but I think they're keeping it from you for a reason."

I cross my arms and give her a look. "Addison, don't make me hurt you."

She laughs. "Seriously, I think they're trying to protect you."

I feel my heart begin to pound. What if something happens to Spike? Or Cade? Whatever they're doing must be dangerous, or they wouldn't be hiding it. Addi notices my expression and reaches out, gripping my arm. "They're going to be fine. They know what they're doing."

"Don't you worry?" I say.

"Every second of every day, but I wanted to be with Cade, and with Cade comes his lifestyle. I can probably deal with it a little easier because I've had a hard life. I know how scary it is for you, with them jumping back in with the man who killed your sister, but they know what they're doing and they won't get hurt."

"What?" I breathe.

184

Her eyes widen and she slaps her hand over her mouth.

"Addison, tell me what you know, now!" I cry. My body shakes.

"Ciara, I didn't mean to say that. Please, it's nothing to worry about."

"It's nothing to worry about?" I cry, leaping to my feet. "He shot my sister in the head, in the middle of a highway. What makes you think he won't do it to Spike just as easily?"

"Spike won't let himself get in that kind of situation again."

"Yes, he will. Going there at all is dangerous."

"I don't even know if they are going there, I just overheard...God, I'm going to get killed. I can't believe I slipped up."

"They're hiding it, because they know I won't agree."

"They're hiding it because they're trying to protect you, honey."

I shake my head. "I don't need protecting."

"Yeah, you do. Spike isn't about to lose someone he loves again. He's not going to let you get close to this."

"It's not me I'm worried about," I sigh, sitting back down. "It's him. If I lose him...after all this..."

"Spike isn't going to get hurt, he's got some serious backup."

I nod, swallowing. Her words don't ease the fear quickly building inside of me. Part of me knew Spike was eventually going to go after the guy who killed Cheyenne, but part of me also hoped he would let it go. I don't blame him for wanting vengeance, anyone would, but the man is dangerous and clearly insane. He doesn't sound like the kind of person anyone should be messing with.

I put my head in my hands, knowing I have to shut my mouth about this. If I go to Spike, guns blazing, he's going to pull away from me. I have to keep what I know under wraps, and then maybe I can figure out if there's a way I can help him.

"Yeah, I know he does," I finally say to Addi. "It's okay. Please don't tell him we had this conversation. He doesn't need extra stress."

Addi actually looks relieved by this. "I am not saying a word."

"Thanks, Addi."

"It'll be ok, honey," she says, patting my hand.

I hope so.

I truly do.

Because, if I lose him again, that's it for me.

There's no coming back a second time.

CHAPTER 15

PRESENT - SPIKE

"Where are we going?" Ciara asks, tightening her grip on my hand.

"You'll see," I say, as we walk down the main street.

I'm taking a big risk, taking her where I'm about to. It'll either go great for me, or it'll ruin any chance I have with her. From what I've seen, the interest is there.

We stop at the start of a large, dark alleyway. I tug her down it, and she hesitates. "It's okay, Tom Cat, I know where I'm going."

"Are you sure?" she whispers.

"Sure, baby, come on."

I walk her down until we find the large, wooden door. I grip the handle and fling it open.

The first thing that greets us is the pounding music. Ciara tilts her head, peering into the massive club we step into. Her eyes widen, and I know why. I turn to her, gauging her reaction. Her cheeks are pink, and her lips are parted slightly. Yeah, she fuckin' loves it.

I walk through the crowd of people, pulling her with me. She hasn't said a word; I think she's in shock. We go through a few doors and I lead her up some stairs until we reach a massive line up of rooms. Bill, an old friend, is standing by the doors.

"Spike, buddy, it's been a long time."

I extend my hand. "Bill, how you been?"

"Good, haven't seen you around here in a while."

"Yeah," I say. "Busy."

"You want a room?"

"Yeah, what you got?"

"Oral, anal, normal."

"Normal. It's her first time."

Ciara makes an odd sound, and her eyes get even wider. I know what she's thinking. She thinks it's a sex club. Downstairs is, technically. People just meet, fuck, drink, fuck, and so on. Upstairs, though, is different. It's for the kinkier minded. Ciara is about to see why.

Bill walks to the second door and he flings it open, extending his hand and ushering us inside. "Enjoy!"

We step into the room, and he closes the door behind us. I lock it, and turn to Ciara. She's looking around the massive, maroon room. Her shoulders drop, and she seems to relax a little, but she hasn't seen the best of it yet. I take her chin, turning her face until she's looking up at me. "I'm trustin' my instincts here, 'cause I am pretty sure you'll like what's behind that curtain, but if you don't, you tell me, yeah?"

"What is this place?" she asks.

"It's a sex club. It's mostly secret, and it's mostly illegal. Owner is in with the cops, and so they stay open. Downstairs is for regulars; they come in, they drink, they fuck, and they leave. Up here is only for a few VIP customers. I'm one of them. I used to come here a lot. You know I have fetishes, Tom Cat, and I think you have the same ones. We're about to find out."

She looks confused, so I turn and walk over the large black curtain covering one wall. I grip the golden tie, and I pull it back.

She takes a few steps backwards, and her cheeks flush a deep red. Her fingers flex, and she looks like she's about to have a panic attack. I'm about to close the curtain, but I can see her expression change slowly, and now it's one of lust. She can't move her eyes away, she's watching, and she's transfixed. I turn, and let my eyes settle on the picture before us.

Behind a large square of one-sided glass is a couple. They're in another room, and while we can see them, they can't see us, but they know we're here. That's the point. They do it because it gets them off, and we do it because it gets us off.

Right now, the two of them are fucking, doggy-style, on the end of the bed. The blonde male is driving his cock in and out of the dark-haired woman's pussy, one hand tangled in her hair, the other slapping her ass until it flushes pink.

"W-w-w-what…" Ciara starts, but she can't say anymore.

I walk over to her, gripping her hand and leading her closer. She steps up to the glass, and she reaches out, putting her fingers to it. "Can they see us?"

"No, babe."

"Do they know we're here?"

"Yeah, babe."

"Why?" she whispers.

"People have fetishes, Tom Cat. Theirs is knowing they're being watched…ours…is watching."

189

She shudders, and presses her face closer to the glass. Taking the opportunity, I press myself up against her back. She trembles, and I run my fingers up her arms, gripping her wrists and raising them above her head. I press her hands flat against the glass, and then run my fingers slowly down her arms until I reach her breasts. I cup them through her top, gently kneading. She tries to hold back the whimper, but it comes out anyway. She's fighting instinct. She knows she likes it, but she's embarrassed that she does.

"You like it baby," I rasp into her ear. "You like watching them fuck just as much as I do. I saw it the other night, I fuckin' felt it. You can deny it, but I can see the way your body responds."

"It's so wrong," she breathes.

"Ain't wrong when they want it."

"I feel dirty."

"And yet you're not, you're so fuckin' sexy."

"You…you…come here a lot?"

"Used to."

"Spike, I don't…I don't…I don't want to like this."

"But baby, you do."

I cup her breast again, and she makes a strangled groaning sound. I lean down, sliding my mouth over her earlobe. "You like watching his cock driving in and out of her wet pussy."

She shudders. "God…"

"You're goin' to come so hard when I touch you. I can feel your nipples hard against my hand. If I put my fingers in your pussy right now, you'd be coming around me in seconds."

190

"Spike," she whimpers. "I don't…"

"You want me to stop, baby, you say the word. You say the word, and I'll turn us around and walk out of this club. It's your call."

I slide my hand down her belly until I reach her pelvis. I press in a little, and she mewls. Fuck. *Yeah.* Her body falls back into mine, and that tells me she wants more, so much more. I run my hands down lower, and dip them into her pants.

She whimpers, and her entire body stiffens. She fuckin' wants it. Every second of it. I slide the tips of my fingers into her panties, and into her wet, sweet folds. She's damp, and fuck, I want to drive so deep inside her right now. She makes a strangled, gasping sound when I find her clit and begin flicking it. She loves it when I flick it. She's got a thing for pain when being given pleasure. Little minx.

"Spike, I…oh god…"

Yeah, that's what I want; her whimpering my name, unable to take her eyes off the couple in front of us. I flick her clit again, and she cries out, shuddering hard. Fuck. Just fuck. She's coming already, and we've just gotten started. She flattens her hands on the glass in front of us, and cries out over and over as her body shakes. I slide a finger insider her, feeling her clenching and pulling around it. Her long blonde hair falls out of its clip, tumbling down her back. I reach one hand up and tangle it through those thick, gorgeous locks and I tug gently. She trembles violently, her body going far and beyond normal release.

"That's just the beginning, baby."

She whimpers again.

I smile.

This should be a fuckin' great night.

~*~*~*~*

PRESENT – CIARA

My body is shaking so hard it feels like I'm having a fit. I'm ashamed of myself for coming so hard, so quickly. Spike is behind me, his big body pressed against mine, his warm lips on my neck, his finger deep inside my pussy. The couple through the glass are fucking so hard, the woman's breasts are bouncing and she's screaming loudly.

I feel my body jerk to life again. I want more. I want him to fuck me, hard against this glass. Then I want him to do it again. I'm so aroused, and part of me feels so incredibly dirty for it, yet the other part is screaming for more. I can't turn my eyes away. I don't know if I even want to.

"Taste how much you fuckin' love it," Spike growls behind me, sliding his finger from my heat and bringing it to my lips.

I suck, he hisses, and we both press harder against the glass. I can feel his throbbing erection on my back, and I'm getting desperate—I want it again.

Spike slips his finger from my mouth and spins me around, pulling me to him and crushing his lips down over mine. We kiss like it's the last kiss we'll ever have, and fuck, it's amazing. Our tongues tangle, our hands grab and pull, our bodies press together desperately. We're in a frenzy, a desperate need-to-fuck-now frenzy.

Spike grips my hair and tugs my head back. Our eyes lock and I can see the ferocity behind his expression. He wants me, and hell, he wants me bad.

193

Slowly he begins sliding down my body, I shiver, knowing what he's going to do, and I want it more than I want his cock right now. When he's on his knees in front of me, he looks up. Fuck, Spike on his knees, looking at me with those beautiful brown eyes, is doing magical things to my body. I reach down, tangle my fingers in his hair, and tug gently. He growls. Spike likes it when I'm rough; he likes it as much as I like it.

I bite my lip, and he makes a rumbling sound. I want to step out of my comfort zone right now, but I'm nervous that he won't like it. Swallowing, and taking a deep breath, I rasp, "Put your mouth on me, Danny."

He groans, and his eyes flare with need. "Baby, fuck, tell me how you want it. Tell me in detail, make me fuckin' see it, feel it, *want* it…"

In a husky voice, I growl, "Put your mouth on my pussy, Danny, and suck. I want you to suck my clit until I'm screaming. I want you to put your fingers inside me, and fuck me so hard I can't stand. I want you all over me."

"Baby," he rasps. "Fuck."

"Now, Danny," I breathe.

His eyes flare with lust, and he has me naked in seconds. When my clothes are tossed aside he grips my ankle, lifting it and putting my foot on his shoulder. Then his mouth is sliding up the inside of my thigh. I tremble, pushing my hips forward and tugging his hair harder. He hisses, and nips my thigh. I groan, god, I'm sick, but that felt fucking amazing. "Do it again, god, bite me again, Spike."

"Danny," he rasps, and then bites my thigh, hard.

I cry out, and throw my head up, letting my eyes settle on the couple on the bed. They are now in the middle of oral sex. The man has his mouth buried deep in the woman's pussy, and she's sucking his dick, hard. I mewl, and Spike keeps climbing higher up my thigh. He snakes his tongue out, tasting me, just touching my swollen flesh. I groan, and jerk my hips again, wanting more. God, I want him to take me hard, in any way he possibly can, and as filthy as he wants. He slides his tongue up my flesh once more, and I growl loudly, like a rabid animal.

"Danny," I groan. "Put your mouth on me, please, put it on me."

He chuckles, and then he slides his mouth over my clit and sucks it into his mouth, hard. I scream, *yep*, scream. I am still watching the couple, and the girl looks how I imagine I look right now. Her head is thrown back, her chest heaving with lust, her nipples hard and protruding. Her body is shaking with desperate need and want. I come hard, so fast it's really shameful, but I can't stop it. I can't even try and stop it. I'm so wound up, I'm so desperate to see more and feel more. I don't want to even think about the guilt of the situation right now, I just want to feel, and fuck, do I feel.

Spike bites my clit again, and he pulls the last of my orgasm from my body. Then he wrenches his mouth away, and slowly gets to his feet.

When he's up, he spins me around, making me face the glass again. My legs wobble, and I reach out and steady myself. Spike leans in close, whispering into my ear, "Spread your legs, now. Hands above your head."

I do as he asks; I spread my legs, and slowly put my hands up above my head. I hear Spike's zipper go, and then I hear him removing his spikes. Jesus, that must get old. He tosses his jacket

195

aside, and I see it land on the large bed in the corner of the room. He shuffles a little more, and then he's behind me, his chest pressing against my back. He moves my hair to one shoulder, and leans down, sliding his tongue up the other until he reaches my ear. "You ready, baby? I'm gonna fuck you so hard, so slow, so deep, you're not going to know which one you want the most. You don't turn your face away from that couple. If you do, I'll spank you. I want dirty talk, I want you tellin' me how fuckin' good it feels, how fuckin' wet you are as I fuck you. Got me?"

"Y-y-yes," I whimper.

"Eyes on them, baby. Tell me what you see right now."

He presses his cock to my pussy, and I struggle to keep my eyes on the couple. I want to close them and groan loudly, but I don't. I stare at the couple moving in front of me, and my body tightens. The man is now behind the woman, kind of like Spike is with me. Except he's got her against a wall, her face smashed against it, and he's got her legs up and over his arms. It's an extremely odd position, but it's also extremely hot. I groan as the man begins sliding his cock in and out of her. That's when Spike drives into me. With one, deep thrust he buries his cock inside me. I cry out, and slap the glass. He growls, and brings his hand around to my front, finding my clit and flicking it.

"Tell me, Tom Cat," he growls into my ear. "What are they doing?"

I know he can see what they're doing, but the fact that he wants me to repeat it makes my body go wild.

"He's...he's fucking her."

"More," he orders.

"He's got her against the wall, oh god," I whimper as Spike tilts his hips, hitting that sweet spot.

"Keep going baby, don't come yet, or I'll pull out."

"He, oh god, he's got her legs in his grip, and he's fucking her from behind."

"Is he fucking her pussy?" Spike growls into her ear.

"Y-y-yes."

"More, Tom Cat."

"He's spanking her, oh…god…oh…more, Spike, please more."

"Tell me more," he hisses. "More, baby."

"His dick is so wet," I pant, zoning my eyes on his cock sliding in and out of the woman's pussy. "God, he's so big. She's wet, I can see her arousal."

"Tell me about *my* cock now, baby," he rasps.

"Your cock is bigger, thicker, harder. Oh god, your cock is perfect."

"Yeah…"

He's fucking me harder now, his hips slamming into my ass. My body is alive, and I'm trying so hard to hold my orgasm back. He's flicking my clit, and fuck, I'm so close. When the man in the other room pulls out of the woman and he comes all over her back, I close my eyes and drop my head, screaming as an orgasm rips through me. Spike slaps my ass so hard; the pain rushes through my body, adding to the orgasm.

"Look at them," he orders, his voice strained, husky, and full of lust.

I raise my head, even though I'm still shaking violently. Spike slaps my ass again, and I find myself begging and rasping, "More."

He does it again and again, and his cock drives in and out, hard.

"Spike, come on me like that," I beg. "God, come on me like that."

I'm watching the man pumping his cock with his fist now, draining the last of his orgasm from it. The woman has his release all over her back, sliding down between her ass cheeks. Spike hisses behind me, and then suddenly he's pulling out. I feel the first spurt of his come on my back, up near my shoulders. I groan as I feel the second and third, hitting me lower and lower each time. Combined with his deep, throaty growls and my own orgasm still being wrung from me, the moment is incredibly erotic. When Spike stops coming, and I stop shuddering, he spins me around and tangles his fingers in my hair. His cock is still hard, and throbbing. My eyes widen.

"You're still so hard."

He laughs hoarsely. "Baby, I will fuck you at least four more times before it goes soft."

What? Oh. My. God.

"Why?"

He reaches down and wraps his fingers around his cock. "Because I fuckin' love it, that's why."

He begins stroking, and my body jumps to life yet again. I turn my eyes to the couple in the other room. They're fucking again. My eyes widen, and my mouth drops open. Spike chuckles, and presses himself up beside me. "He takes Viagra so he can fuck her all night."

"God, he must be tired," I whisper.

"No, baby, he's full of lust and need. Like me."

"Are you going to fuck me all night?" I whimper, turning to face him.

"Babe, I'm going to fuck you until the sun is shining."

I swallow, and suddenly feel like a tiny, fragile little girl. Spike is looking at me like he wants to eat me alive, and shit; it's both scary and thrilling. He steps toward me, and I find myself stepping back.

"Baby, you don't wanna fuck, you just say so…"

I do want to fuck. Oh, I do. I just want to play first. I smile, and step back again. Grinning, he walks toward me, looking like a tiger about to lunge. I keep backing up until I'm pressed up against the glass. He stops in front of me, flashing me that gorgeous smile. "Tom Cat wants to play. Tell me, how do you wanna play?"

"I want to do what they do…"

Spike's eyes widen. "You wanna copy?"

"I wanna copy."

"Baby, fuck…"

I grin. "Yeah, fuck. Can you handle it, Danny?"

He grins, looking like a man on a mission. "Baby, I can handle it."

We both turn, and stare at the couple in the other room. My cheeks flush, and my body grows hot. Right now, she's on her knees sucking him. I turn to Spike, and he grins and points to his cock. "Away you go, baby."

I drop to my knees, wrapping my hand around the base of his cock. He hisses, and I take my time bringing him to my lips. I swirl my tongue up and down his shaft, and over his balls, before taking him into my mouth. When I do, the sound he makes is primal, and all male. He grips the sides of my face and gently works himself in and out of my mouth. He groans, and I smile around him. I love having the control, even just for a second. I suck and lick, enjoying the moment, tasting our lust on him. With a pained groan, Spike slides his cock from my mouth and stands me up. I realize it's because the couple has moved. Now, the man has the girl on his lap in a chair, and she's riding him.

I put my hands on Spike's chest, and I shove him toward the chair in the corner. He drops down on it, and I climb onto his lap. His eyes are on mine, and fuck; the expression on his face right now is enough to take my breath away, permanently.

He grips my hips, lowering me down onto his cock. As he slowly sinks into me, we both groan. I grip his hair, pushing my chest out and bringing my nipple to his mouth. He leans down, wrapping his lips around it and sucking softly. I whimper, and turn my face to the couple. The expression on the other man's face is very similar to Spike's.

I begin rocking on Spike's cock, and his groan vibrates through my body. My body burns with the need for another release, I begin rocking harder, feeling myself clenching around Spike.

"Spike, I hate that I need to come, but fuck, I need to come," I whisper, hoarsely.

He removes his mouth from my nipple, and tilts my hips. Then he drives up into me, hard and fast, taking over the movement. I come again, screaming and thrashing as my orgasm, better than the last, rips through me. Spike makes a throaty, desperate sound, and suddenly we're up. My legs are wrapped around his hips, and his mouth is on mine. He kisses me with such ferocity my head spins.

He walks me to the bed, and he pulls out of me, putting me down and flipping me onto my stomach. I turn my head again, seeing the other couple is also doing this. Spike grips my hips, tilting them up, and then he drives into me again. I cry out, and drop my head into the soft mattress. Spike thrusts and thrusts, slapping my ass every now and then, as well as tugging my hair. I come twice more before he comes along with me.

"Tom Cat," he roars, exploding inside of me.

I let him ride out his orgasm, before dropping my body into the bed. I'm exhausted. God, I don't know how he does it. Spike pulls out of me, and flops down beside me on the bed. We both lay for a minute, panting.

He rolls onto his side and stares down at me. I turn my head, giving him a weak smile, to which he reaches across and strokes a piece of hair from my face.

"Not goin' to fuck you anymore, baby."

I pout, and he chuckles.

"You'll have to miss more days of work, 'cause you won't be able to walk."

He makes a valid point. I smile, too tired to even try and speak.

"When did you change so much, Tom Cat…"

I open my mouth and whisper, "Maybe I was like that all along—you just didn't get a chance to see it."

His eyes soften, and they slide over my face before going back up to meet mine. "Yeah, maybe."

"Can I sleep now? Please don't tell me I have to get dressed and leave," I groan.

He chuckles. "Sorry baby, we gotta run. We're stayin' the night and will be back before your shift tomorrow. You can go back to my hotel and sleep if you want, I gotta do some shit."

"Sounds good to me," I whisper, stretching.

He nods. "Hey babe, you are on birth control, right?"

I shake my head, what the hell? How random. I open my mouth to answer with a yes, when I realize that I haven't been keeping up-to-date with my birth control shot. My stomach leaps into my throat, and I close my mouth quickly. Shit! What was I thinking? How could I be so stupid? I struggle to remain calm. It's fine, it's probably not even run out yet. I'm probably over reacting.

"Ciara?" Spike asks.

"I…um, yeah, it's fine."

"Fuck," he hisses. "Fuck, Ciara! Why didn't you tell me you weren't on it? I fucked you bareback."

I see the look on his face, and it hits me hard and fierce. Spike doesn't want babies. I can see it all over his face, his eyes are wide and alert, and his jaw is tense with emotion. My heart dies a little, and I'm so hurt. God, it burns. Not because he doesn't want it, just that he's looking at me like I'm about to rip his heart out again. I swallow, and force my face to become impassive.

202

"It's fine, I'm on an injection. I just had an STD freak attack then, that's all."

Relief washes over him. Fuck. Shit. What am I going to do? I'm going to go home and make sure I'm up-to-date, but something deep down inside me is making me think I'm no longer protected. I try to do the math in my head, and as far as I know, I haven't updated it. God, I feel sick.

"I don't have STDs babe, I use condoms."

Well, that's one less thing to worry about.

"Ciara?" he asks.

I turn my eyes to his. "I'm fine, sorry. I just can't believe I didn't ask you that."

He reaches across and touches my face. "I wouldn't fuck you without protection if I knew I wasn't careful in the past. Cheyenne is the only woman."

I swallow, nodding.

"You're not okay," he points out.

"I am, sorry, I just had a mild panic attack," I say softly.

"Because of the STDs or because of the fact I said I didn't want babies?"

I flinch.

"Fuck, Ciara."

"It's okay," I say, my voice wobbling. "I understand. We shouldn't even be talking about this right now, we're not even together."

He looks hurt now. Fuck.

"Then what are we?"

"We're trying, remember?"

"I'm sorry if my words hurt, Ciara, but there ain't no way in hell I ever want kids…not after Cheyenne died, carryin' my baby. I just don't wanna ever feel that again."

I'm crushed. My soul, it burns. I force myself to nod and smile, but inside I feel like I am being ripped to pieces.

"I'm really tired, can we go?"

His face tightens. "Ciara, fuck, if there's going to be a problem…"

"It's okay," I say, smiling even though I'm hurting inside. "I'm okay with that, I know how you feel. I'm sorry, it all just came as a shock. We're okay."

He narrows his eyes again, but nods. "All right, let's go."

We both stand and dress ourselves. My heart is throbbing, and my body feels wobbly. What if I'm already pregnant?

Shit.

What do I do then?

CHAPTER 16

PRESENT – CIARA

I tell Spike I need to get something back to Addi, and I ask him if he can drop me off to their hotel room. He agrees, saying he needs to speak with Cade anyway. The entire ride is silent, and my head is spinning.

When we arrive at the hotel, I jump off the bike and rush through the gates. Spike follows me, his boots crunching heavily on the rocks. Cade, Jackson, and Addison are all standing outside near the pool, just under the bright, blue light that shines down onto the water. Cade nods at Spike, and smiles at me. Addi notices my expression and walks over quickly. I grip her arm, flashing Cade, Jackson and Spike a fake smile.

"I just need to borrow Addi, real quick."

They all watch me, confused. Spike's eyes narrow, and he crosses his arms. I spin Addi around and we walk off. When we get around the side of the building, I burst into a fit of uncontrollable tears.

"Hey, whoa, Ciara…what's wrong," Addi says, pulling me into her arms.

"I think I have a massive problem."

"What happened?"

I tell her what went down between Spike and I, then I step back, swiping my eyes to gauge her reaction.

"Shit," she says, sighing deeply.

"I don't know what to do, Addi. I know I could be jumping ahead, but we've had a lot of sex and…well…most of it's been unprotected. I'm such an idiot, at the time I didn't even think."

"Hey, it's not just you who didn't think, honey."

"He won't stick around. If I'm pregnant, he's going to run."

"All right, all right, let's think about this. You two haven't been together more than a few days, yeah?"

I nod. "Yeah."

"Well, there is the option of the morning after pill."

I swallow, and begin crying even harder. "God, Addi, this sucks."

"You might not even be pregnant, but if it's something you are really worried about, you might want to consider your options. The morning after stops it before it happens, and right now I think it's the best choice. You and Spike are rocky, you haven't been together long enough to deal with something like that, even if there's only a small chance. You have to think about what you want more."

"It's him," I whisper. "It's always been him."

"Then we'll go for a drive, yeah?"

I nod, swallowing.

"Come here," she says, pulling me into her arms. We hug for a long moment, before she pulls back and wipes my face with a tissue she pulls from her purse.

"Thank you, Addi."

"Anytime, honey. Come on, we'll say we're hungry. That'll work."

It's already well into the night, so I'm sure that won't work that well, but it's worth a shot. I swipe my eyes again, and we walk back out to join the guys. I avoid staring at Spike as Addi speaks, but I can feel his eyes on me.

"Hey, we're going to get something to eat, let you guys talk."

"You just ate, babe," Cade points out.

"Well, Ciara is hungry, so I'll just get a coffee."

"You never said you were hungry," Spike says, his voice hard.

"I…um…I just got hungry."

"A word, Ciara?" he says, gripping my arm and pulling me out of everyone else's hearing range.

When we stop, he turns to me. "What the fuck is goin' on?"

I cross my arms, staring at my shoes. "Nothing, we're just going to get something to eat."

"Look at me."

"Spike, can we not do this now because…"

"Look at me, now," he growls.

I lift my head, and do as he says. His eyes flash with emotion, and he narrows them, confused. "You've been cryin'? Why? Did I hurt you?"

"No, I'm fine."

"You're fuckin' lyin' to me!" he snarls.

"I am not!" I cry, crossing my arms.

"Is this 'cause I said I didn't want kids, 'cause fuck, Ciara…I was only bein' honest."

I spit it, yep, like a great big child. "It's got nothing to do with that! It's got everything to do with the fact that I'm not on protection. I lied, Spike. I lied when I said I was. I'm not, and you fucked me without being careful. Then you proceeded to tell me you never want kids. So I'm going to the fuckin' pharmacy to get a pill to make sure I'm not. Got it?"

I spin around and storm off before he can stop me. He bellows my name, but I don't stop. I get to Addi, grip her arm and pull her towards the road.

"Ciara!" Spike yells, running after me, his heavy boots pounding on the pavement.

"Come on," I say, tugging Addi harder.

We get onto the street, and wave down a cab. Luckily for us, one stops. We both climb in and close the doors. The cab just pulls out as Spike steps out of the hotel grounds. He's cursing loudly; I can see his lips moving, as he drives his fist into a nearby tree. I close my eyes and turn them away. Addi stares at him, confused, and then looks at me. "What happened?"

"He got up me, I lost it and told him what we're doing."

Addi turns and looks at him again before we disappear around the street. "He doesn't look happy about it."

"He's just pissed off because I lied to him."

"Are you sure about that, honey?"

I swallow. God, what if I'm wrong? I shake my head. "God, no…"

"Maybe we should stop…"

"No, it's okay. It's for the best, regardless. Like you said, we're not ready for something like that. It wouldn't end well."

"Are you sure?"

I nod, feeling my knees wobble. We round another corner, and Addi turns and stares out the window. "Shit."

I turn, and see Spike coming up behind us at a rapid speed on his bike. Shit. I turn to Addi, eyes wide. "What is he doing?"

"I guess he doesn't want you to go and get that pill."

"Far out, what do I do?"

"I don't know," she says, her eyes wide. "Pull over?"

Spike pulls up alongside of the cab, and pulls out a gun. The cabbie screeches and skids to an abrupt stop, causing both Addi and I to fall forward in our seats. Thank god for seatbelts.

Spike leaps off his bike, drops it on its stand, opens the door, unbuckles my seat belt and hauls me out and onto the street. People honk their horns and skid around us. I gasp and squirm, but Spike's grip is unmovable. Addi sits in the back of the cab, eyes wide, and the driver is praying, yes, praying.

"You," Spike growls to the driver. "Take her back where you came from."

He nods frantically, and the car surges forward. Addi leans out the window and yells, "Sorry honey!"

209

Spike shoves me toward his bike and growls, "Fuckin' get on, now!"

I do. I don't dare argue.

I get on the back and pull the helmet on quickly. He jumps on the front and takes off so fast I scream. He zips in and out of cars angrily, and I can see the knuckles on his right hand are bleeding. My heart pounds, and I hold on for dear life. He's riding like a maniac.

He skids to a stop at a small beach, and gets off the bike. I follow, with wobbling legs. He storms down onto the sand, his body rigid. I hesitantly walk down after him, not knowing what sort of reaction he's going to have. He spins when I stop behind him, and I can see he's panting.

"You might have my fuckin' baby inside you, and you were goin' to fuckin' kill it?"

I gasp. "What? No!"

"Yes, you fuckin' were."

"I..." God what can I say? "I thought, you said you never wanted..."

"I don't!" he bellows. "I'd never go outta my way to have a baby, but fuck, do you think I'm such a cunt that I wouldn't be there for someone if I knocked them up? Fuck, Ciara, you give me no credit. I'd never fuckin' leave you alone, not ever."

I start to cry. I wrap my arms around my belly, and look at the sand. "You said you didn't want kids, it's a pain you couldn't feel again. I freaked out; I didn't know what to do. It was the only thing I could think of, that would save us both the pain. I didn't want to lose you and…"

"You read me wrong," he interrupts. "I know what I said, and I meant it. If I had a choice, I wouldn't have kids because it fuckin' burns to lose them, but this ain't a choice and therefore it can't be changed. If you were pregnant by accident, then I would never leave you alone. I'd always be there. I'm not a fuckin' asshole, Ciara. I might not want it right now, but fuck, I'd make sure it had the best life ever. You have to understand that."

I look up at him, and hot tears flood my cheeks. "I didn't want to hurt you."

"It was my fuckin' fault, too. I didn't ask until after I fuckin' came inside you, numerous times. It wasn't on you, and it shouldn't be left on you. I don't like that you fuckin' lied to me when I asked, but I know why you did it. There ain't no pill gettin' taken. There ain't no way in shit I am willingly killing a child that may be inside you. Fuck, no, Ciara."

"I'm sorry."

He nods, stiffly. "Yeah, I get that."

"But you're hurt…"

"Fuck, of course I am. You and the rest of the fuckin' world keep on thinkin' that you know me so well."

"The sad thing is," I whisper, my voice low, "is that I know you, better than most, and I still jumped to conclusions."

"Yeah, you fuckin' did."

"I'm sorry."

"I know you are," he sighs. "When are you goin' to know?"

I swallow, and look away toward the ocean. "In a few weeks."

"Right, well, til' then we'll use protection."

"Spike?"

He meets my gaze as I turn back to him.

"I know you don't want this, so why are you trying to support me?"

"I'm not a cunt, Ciara. I don't want it right now, but I'll deal with it and I'll make the best of it, if that's what I need to do."

I nod, and watch him turn and walk toward his bike. He's hurting; I can see it written all over him.

I hang my head, and I follow him. He's already on it, the engine grumbling beneath him. I climb on the back, pull my helmet on and wrap my arms around him. He takes off into the night, and I struggle to fight back the tears the entire way back to the hotel.

When we pull up, I get off the bike and he follows. Neither of us speak as we walk in and over to where Cade, Jackson, Granger, Muff and Addison are sitting. They all give us weary expressions.

"Need to talk with you boys. Addison, Ciara, leave," Spike says, his voice empty and angry.

Addi's eyes widen, but she stands. I don't move.

"Spike," I begin.

"You fuckin' heard me, Ciara. Ain't none of your fuckin' business what I'm about to say, and considerin' you ain't my Old

212

Lady, you don't get a right to argue it. Now fuckin' leave. I'll be up later."

"Spike, you asshole!" Addi snaps.

Spike gives her a look so fierce, she steps back. Cade stands and puts a hand on Spike's shoulder, giving him a silent warning to slow down. Then he turns to us, giving me a soft expression. "Go up with Addi, yeah? We won't be long."

I don't answer him, or look at Spike. I just turn and walk off with Addi. My heart is throbbing, but I don't look back.

Addi takes me up to my room, and when we're inside, she turns to me. "You okay?"

I shrug, but my heart aches. "Yeah, I'm okay."

"He's just hurting."

"He's angry, because he doesn't want me to be pregnant, yet he doesn't want to feel guilty if he asks me to take that pill."

"He's probably just reliving some old memories. Give him some space."

She's probably right, so I don't bother to argue. I turn to her, and give her a weak smile. "I'm not trying to be rude, but do you mind if I just go to bed?"

She smiles, and nods. "Of course. Hey, you will call if you need me, yeah?"

"Yeah," I say.

She hugs me, and then she's gone. I turn and stare at the room, with its crappy green walls, old brown carpet and curtains that have seen better days, and then, with a sigh I walk into the shower. I stand

213

in the warm water for what seems like hours, and then I get out and dress myself, before crawling into bed. I lay on the soft, thick pillow thinking of Spike's words, unable to get them out of my head. They hurt, a lot.

You're not even my Old Lady.

Ouch.

CHAPTER 17

PRESENT – SPIKE

"You know you're too fuckin' angry to deal with this right now," Cade says, giving me a look.

"No, I'm not," I growl. "Now tell me what you know."

"Spike, buddy, have a drink and sit yeah?" Granger says, shoving a beer at me.

I take it and pop the top, before bringing it to my lips and swallowing. It does help, and with each sip, I feel calmer. Fuck, what was I thinking, speaking to Ciara like that? It was fucked up. She didn't deserve that, not at all. It ain't her fault she's in this position, it's equally mine. I just reacted so badly, givin' her mixed signals. She got abused for wanting to take that pill, then she got shoved away because she didn't take it.

Fuck, I'm a cunt. Seriously, a cunt. I swallow more beer, and then I turn to the group. We came to the city to get the final information on our deal with Hogan's men. We finally got it too, we got some of his contacts. Now all we have to do is send someone in to make a deal, and then we have his location.

"I'm good," I say. "Tell me what we've got."

"We got his inside sources, now all we gotta do is make the deal," Granger says.

"Who are we sendin' in?"

"One of my guys, Junior," Cade says.

"Can he be trusted?" I ask, pulling out a cigarette and lighting it.

"Yeah, he's shown his loyalty."

I nod. "When's he goin' in?"

"He's making contact with the guy tonight. We should know more by morning."

"What's our plan of action once we get the location of Hogan?" Jackson asks.

"Are we going in as a stealth attack, or an all-out brawl?" Granger asks.

"He's got quite a club. We can't risk just jumpin' in for the attack. We have to be smart about it," I say.

Jackson crosses his arms. "If we kill him, we're going to end up with a fuck load of members after us."

I nod. "That's why we're gonna be discreet. I'm thinkin' a car bomb."

"You wanna fuckin' blow the club?" Cade asks, horrified.

"Yeah, I wanna blow the fuckin' club. If we can make sure he's in it, then we can make sure him and a mass of his guys are taken down in one hit."

"It's not a bad idea," Muff says. "It will reduce numbers."

"And keep us anonymous," Granger adds.

"You don't think he's goin' to know it was you?" Cade asks.

"He might, but he'll be dead," I snort.

Cade laughs. "Yeah, what about the other guys?"

"No, I doubt it."

216

"So we go in, plant a car and just blow it?" Jackson says.

"Yeah."

"What about Old Ladies?" Granger adds.

"What about them?" I growl. "He didn't care about shootin' my wife's brains out. I'm not goin' to fuckin' think about his. This is fuckin' war, it ain't a walk in the fuckin' park."

Granger nods. "No problems, Prez. Cool it."

"I'm going to see Ciara, you boys keep me updated with the deal tonight."

I stand and crush out my cigarette.

"On it," Cade says.

They all nod at me, and I turn and walk toward my room. When I get in Ciara is curled up in bed, out to the world, lookin' a cute as a fuckin' kitten. I feel like a jerk.

I walk over, stopping beside the bed and starin' down at her. She's breathing deeply, her blonde hair fanned out over the pillow. I know I hurt her tonight, and I'll make up for it. I won't let her think this is on her, 'cause it ain't. I shrug out of my jacket, and then I strip out of my clothes. My cock is raw from all the fucking I've been doing, but shit, I'd go again. Ciara, she's a wildcat. Fuck, I never knew she was so adventurous.

When I'm naked, I pull the sheets back and climb into the bed. Ciara groans and moves.

I press my lips to her shoulder, and she whimpers.

Time to make it better.

~~*~*~

PRESENT – CIARA

I feel hot lips against my shoulder, and I slowly wake up. I can feel the heat coming from Spike's body, so I know he's in the bed with me. I feel his finger slide up and down the skin on my arm, gently, softly.

I flutter my eyes open, and the dim light in the room makes me blink. I turn my face, and see Spike lying next to me, his brown eyes on mine. He looks soft, gentle, sweet and not the man who just told me to fuck off. He leans down, pressing his lips to my throat, and I find myself tilting my head back and letting him. He slides his lips down over my shoulder and then he lifts my shirt up and over my head. I let him, though I'm not even sure why.

"Ciara," he murmurs against my skin, as he slides his mouth over my breast. "So fuckin' sorry baby, I was a cunt."

I shudder at his words, and my body instantly forgives him when his mouth reaches the heated flesh between my legs. He spreads my thighs and then his tongue is inside me, sliding up and down my clit. I groan, and tangle my fingers in the sheets, tilting my hips up to meet his feverish licking. He sucks and nips, rolling my clit around with his tongue. He slides two fingers inside me, gently stretching my sore, sensitive flesh. He slides them out and back in, slowly, gently. I cry out, and my body tightens around his fingers as he sucks my clit harder, flicking and teasing.

"Spike," I whimper as I begin to come.

My body spirals up and out of control, and my orgasm tears through me like wildfire. Spike growls against my flesh as he slides

218

his fingers in and out of my damp pussy, and his tongue continues dancing on my clit.

I stop shuddering when my orgasm subsides, and Spike gently removes himself from me, and slides back up my body. He grips my arms, rolling me into his side as he lies down on the pillow beside me. I curl into him, pressing my face against his skin and sliding my tongue out and over the hard, delicious flesh on his chest. He growls as I slide my other hand down his body to find his cock, hard and pulsing. I wrap my fingers around it, and begin to stroke it gently.

"Baby," he rasps. "You don't need to touch me. I didn't do that for me, I did it for you."

"I want to," I whisper.

"I was an ass, you should be snapping it off not…fuck…"

I squeeze his cock, cutting his sentence short. Then I begin gently massaging it again. I can feel the spikes against my fingertips; the tops of them press into my skin, but I don't care. I keep stroking him, up and down, up and down. Every now and then I stop and give his head a little squeeze. His breathing has become harsher, and his body is wound up tight. I keep stroking, pumping my fist harder. It aches, but I don't want to stop. I will myself to keep going. I want to feel him come in my hand, I want to know that I can get him there just by doing this.

"Baby," he pants. "Goin' to come."

I jerk him harder, and then I feel his cock swell in my hand before hot spurts of come shoot out and coat my hand and his pelvis. I can feel his cock pulsing as each warm spurt releases. He releases only one groan, the rest of the time he lies with his head back, his jaw tight and his body shaking. Lovely.

When his cock begins to soften in my hand, I let him go. I pull my hand out, and reach over to the table beside me and pick up a towel. I wipe myself, and then I pull the sheets back and wipe him. He shudders again, and stares over at me, his expression content.

"Did they hurt?" I ask, as I lift his cock and wipe all around it. My fingers once again graze the piercings.

"The dick rings?"

"Yeah."

He nods. "Fuck yeah."

"Why the spikes?"

He shrugs as I drop the towel and pull the sheets back over us, and nestle myself back into his arms.

"Liked the idea of havin' somethin' different. Then I fucked a girl one night who made a point of takin' them all out, and so it started."

"You got them done back when I knew you, and you never told me."

"Didn't think it was somethin' you would want to hear, Tom Cat."

"True," I laugh softly. "I would have blushed until I exploded."

He laughs. "Yeah, you would have."

We lay silent for a moment, and then he looks to me and says, "I'm sorry for speakin' to you like that earlier. I was a jerk."

"Yeah, you were."

He grins. "Am I forgiven?"

"Aren't you always?"

He pulls me closer, squeezing tightly. "You're too fuckin' good for me, Tom Cat."

"That might be how you see it," I whisper, feeling my eyes grow heavy. "But it's certainly not how I see it."

"Changin' everything," he says quietly.

If only he knew, he was changing everything, too.

My entire world is different because of him.

CHAPTER 18

PRESENT – CIARA

"Tom Cat, hurry up and finish, my cock is burning for you," Spike whispers into my ear.

I grin and spin, gripping his arms and bringing his lips to mine for a deep kiss. The music around us is pounding. It's a Saturday night at the bar and I'm working, as always. Spike came in earlier, and has been patiently waiting for me to finish. Add in some dirty talk, and he's officially got me worked up. He pulls back from our kiss, flashing me a grin that has my panties melting. Fuck that grin. He's gorgeous.

"Ciara?"

That voice. Even over the music, it has my blood running cold. Spike knows it, too, because his entire body stiffens. Letting me go, we both turn to see my mother and father standing in the entryway. Oh. Shit.

I haven't seen them since the day I ran off, nor have I heard from them, so seeing them here is a complete shock. I don't know why they're here, and I'm not even sure I want to. My mother, once beautiful, looks worn. Her blonde hair is dull, her blue eyes lifeless. My father, usually tall and broad, is slumping and his dark hair is filled with gray. Their eyes scan Spike and I, and for a moment, my world stops. I know how badly this is going to go down.

"Mom…Dad…" I whisper.

My father's eyes are on Spike, and the look he's giving him is that of pure hate. I step forward, my legs wobbly, until I stop in front of them. "W-w-what are you doing here?"

222

"How could you?" my mother shrieks.

I flinch. "It's…"

My father lifts his hand, and before I realize what's happening, it connects with my face in an almighty slap that has the entire bar grinding to a halt. My ears ring and my eyes water as my head swings to the side and I lose my footing. I stumble to the floor, smashing into a heap of tables and people.

People quickly help, reaching down and lifting me. It takes me a moment to clear my vision and when I do, I see Spike standing, fists clenched, panting with rage.

"How could you?" my mother screams.

I get to my feet, my knees wobbly, my face burning. I cup my cheek, and I open my mouth and rasp out, "I know it looks bad, but…"

"But what?" she screams. "You're a whore! You're a filthy whore!"

Spike lunges forward, but I manage to step in front of him.

"You ever fuckin' speak to her like that again and I'll put you on your ass!" he roars.

"You lowlife piece of shit," my dad bellows. "She's dead and you're moving on to her sister. Is that all you think of my daughter? Is that all she meant to you?"

"She meant the motherfuckin' world to me, but she's gone and I can't live the rest of my life alone."

"So you pick her sister?" my dad hisses. "You disgusting piece of trash. It should have been you that died. I should have done it myself!"

"Dad!" I cry.

He turns his gaze to me. "*You.* You're nothing but a slut. I am ashamed to call you my daughter. My beautiful Cheyenne is dead because of the two of you, and how do you honor her memory? You fuck her husband."

His words bring me to my knees. I slowly sink down, feeling my body heave with emotion.

"You best fuckin' leave!" Spike growls. "Now."

"I hope you're proud of yourself!" my mother screeches. "I hope you know what you've done. We came back to make things better, and we find you running around with your dead sister's husband. You are disgusting."

I cover my face and shake my head. My emotions are a mix of anger and frustration. I lift my face from my hands, and I meet her stony cold, blue eyes.

"I am proud of myself," I scream so loudly that the entire bar goes silent. "I am proud of everything I've done, and that includes him." I jab a finger at Spike. "He's everything to me, and he was everything to me before Cheyenne came along. If you want to hate me, go right ahead. It's not like I haven't lived my entire life with the same emotion being tossed at me on a daily basis.

"I'm sorry Cheyenne is gone, but it isn't my fault. It was never my fault. She wanted Spike, she pushed for him, and you can blame me as much as you want for that but she was a big girl and she made her own choices. I'll never be sorry for being with him now, because

224

I love him. I've loved him far longer than she did, and I'll love him until I stop breathing. Maybe it's wrong, maybe it's disgusting, but it's my happiness and you know what?" I get to my feet, my legs shaking. "I fucking deserve it!"

Then, with legs that don't want to move, I walk out of the bar. I get to the parking lot before they catch up with me. My mother grips my arm and swings me around, her face wild with emotion.

Then suddenly, she lets me go. Her eyes widen and she takes a few steps backwards. I turn slowly, and see what she sees: Spike, Cade, Granger, Muff and about ten other bikers are standing in a massive line, glaring at her. She stumbles backwards, and clutches my father's arm. Spike steps forward until he's in their faces.

"You ever lay a motherfucking hand on her again, I'll kill you," he hisses at my father, and then he turns to my mother. "And if you ever call her another trashy name, I'll knock you the fuck out. I will only say this once, so you fuckin' listen, and listen good. Cheyenne made her fuckin' choices, and her choice was me. She put herself in my life, and she chose to stay there. Ain't Ciara's doing, and it wasn't my doing.

"I loved your daughter, I loved her with everything I knew how to love with at the time. I took care of her, and then I fucked up, and she's gone because of me. I'm not sayin' I'll ever forgive myself for that, 'cause I won't, but it can't be undone.

"As for her—" He points a finger at me. "—she's been my fuckin' heart since the day I laid eyes on her. She's been treated like a fuckin' dog by you two and her sister, and she didn't deserve that. You have done wrong by her, and you fuckin' know it. You will never admit it though, because you're too fuckin' selfish. You can call me every name under the sun, you can disown her and treat her like a dog, and you can think whatever you want about the situation,

225

but the reality is that I fuckin' love Ciara, and I've loved her from the moment I laid eyes on her. Don't mean I didn't love Cheyenne, 'cause I fuckin' did, it just means I probably didn't love her as much as she deserved, and she did fuckin' deserve it.

"The truth of the matter is that my heart has, and always will, belong to Ciara and there ain't no fuckin' way I'm livin' another second without her because of shit that went on in the past."

I'm crying, I mean I am blubbering and clutching my chest, staring at Spike and wanting to wrap myself around him and never let go. My mother pokes her nose to the sky and humphs, and my father stares at the bikers forming a line behind us. He turns to me, his eyes glassy with rage and part of me would like to hope, emotion. "If this is what you want, fine, Ciara," he says. "But we won't be a part of it."

I swallow and stand up tall, walking over and taking Spike's hand. "You never have been part of it."

He stares at me, and then turns and takes my mother's arm. She glares at me for a long moment and then turns and walks off with him. Just like that, my family leaves me, again.

Then I think of the people behind me, and I realize I've had the family I wanted all along. I turn to Spike, and he looks down at me, his brown eyes full of love and admiration. He lifts his hand, and he strokes my throbbing cheek.

"You love me," I whisper.

"Yeah," he rasps. "I was just a fuckhead and didn't tell you sooner."

I smile through my tears, through my pain - through it all that smile breaks through. "You make me happy, Danny. Forever."

226

He leans down, gripping my face and pressing his lips to mine.

"Yeah babe, I fuckin' know."

"Take me home. I want in your bed until I can't walk."

He flashes me a devilish grin. "Babe, you know me too well."

He grips my hand and turns to the guys. "You boys enjoy your night, and thanks. Tell Joe Ciara has gone home too, yeah?"

They all nod at him, and then turn and walk into the bar. Spike takes my hand and leads me to his bike. I climb on happy, content and feeling like finally, I might have a chance to make something of my life.

And finally, it's with the man I adore.

Fuck yeah.

CHAPTER 19

PRESENT – CIARA

"Hey Addi, is Spike here?" I call to Addi as I walk through the Hell's Knights compound two weeks later.

"He's in with Cade, two doors on the left honey."

"Thank you! I'll come chat when I'm done, I just have to ask him about something."

She waves a hand and flashes me a grin. I return it, and then head down the hall.

I smile as I walk, finally happy. Spike and I have been going great for the past few weeks. I spend most nights with him, and we spend a lot of time fucking. Oh, and what great fucking it is. I feel my cheeks heat as I move down the large hall. We haven't found out if I'm pregnant or not yet, and I think we have kind of stopped worrying about it. At least, I have.

I grip the handle to the door that is second on the left, like Addison said. I knock, but no one answers, so with a shrug, I open it. What I see has me reeling back into the hall, screaming at the top of my lungs.

Jackson, one of his MC members, and a pretty blonde girl. Fucking. I mean...hardcore, fucking. Jackson is behind her driving in and out, and his MC friend is having his cock sucked. Oh. My. God! I scrub at my eyes and swing my head from side to side, mumbling 'No, no, no, no, no,' over and over. Jackson calls out my name, but I can't scrub the image from my mind. Jackson, my father-like figure, my kind, sweet Jackson...was sharing. He was having a ménage. Jackson...JACKSON. Oh god, it burns.

I can't erase the images no matter how hard I try. Jackson skids out of the room, jeans up but unbuttoned, bulge...well...bulging. I squeal, and cover my eyes.

"Jackson, oh my GOD!"

"Ciara, shit, fuck, sorry...I didn't lock the door..."

"Oh god, my eyes, they burn. Oh my god!"

"What's goin' on?"

That's Spike.

"Ciara, um, walked in on me and..."

"Oh god!" I cry again, turning and rushing down the hall.

"Sorry!" Jackson yells.

I tear out into the bar, and Addi calls my name. "Ciara, hey, what's wrong?"

I look up at her, my eyes wide and no doubt freaked out. "Um, um..."

She walks around the bar, looking concerned. "What's wrong, are you okay?"

"Um, ah..."

"Ciara..."

"Tom Cat!" Spike calls, walking out into the bar, smirking.

"Don't you even laugh!"

Addison looks confused. "What's going on?"

Spike walks over to her, wrapping his arm around her shoulders. "Precious, trust me when I say you don't wanna know."

"Tell me!" she cries, stomping her foot with frustration.

Spike squeezes her harder. "Seriously, you don't wanna know."

"Ciara, hey!"

I turn and see Jackson walking out, still without a shirt. My eyes widen, and I throw up my hands. "No, it's fine. It's fine."

"I'm sorry, I feel like a fucking dog…"

"What happened?!" Addi cries loudly.

"Ciara walked in on me…ummm…" As if just realizing what he was about to say to his daughter, he stops talking. "Errr…"

"Oh my God, did Ciara catch you fucking?" Addison bellows.

Trust her to put it so…*bluntly*.

"She caught him with more than one person," Spike chuckles.

I slap Spike's shoulder and he grunts, but flashes me an amused grin, that smart-ass. Addison squeals loudly, and begins gagging, fake of course.

"Oh my God! Father! You are so gross! You're like…a whore!"

"It's not…" Jackson begins.

"Hey, the man likes to share with his buddies, nothin' wrong with that," Spike says.

I slap his arm again. "Spike!"

"Father," Addison cries, covering her eyes. "That's so wrong! Oh my god, are you Bi?"

Jackson snorts. "No fuckin' way. I don't touch the other man, we just fuckin'…share a woman…"

"Jackson, good on you buddy!" Spike laughs.

Addison and I both shoot him a glare now. Jackson runs a hand through his hair again, and sighs loudly. "Fuck it, I'm goin' back in!"

Addison and I both squeal loudly, and then we're all laughing. Jackson disappears off down the hall, and we continue on with our laughing.

Well that was a way to end the day.

Dammit.

~*~*~*~

PRESENT – SPIKE

"We ride in a hour, have everything ready," I bark down the phone, and snap it closed.

I glance over my shoulder. Ciara is still in the bedroom, thank fuck. If she found out what we were planning, she would have a fit. She thinks we're going on an annual ride, and she's totally okay with that. I hate lying to her, but if she knew what I was going to do, she wouldn't make it easy on me.

I know she won't understand, I don't expect her to, but I have to do this for Cheyenne. She deserves that much. I need closure, and making him pay will give that to me.

231

The plan is set in place. It's taken a few weeks, but it's finally ready to go. Our boy is going to drive the car in the compound to get the deal, then he's going to walk off as though he's double-checking on the phone and we're going to blow the entire place. We've made sure to follow Hogan's every move, so we know he'll be on the inside.

I turn, taking my pack from the ground, and then I walk into the bedroom. Ciara is sitting by the window, smiling out at something. God knows what, the girl is always sunshine, even if she can't see it.

She turns when she hears me, and she beams. Fuck, I love her. I love her with every beat of my broken fuckin' heart. I walk over, cupping her face in my hands. I bring my lips down to hers and I kiss her, hard. She tastes like some fuckin' sweet strawberry lip stuff. It's nice, whatever it is. She opens her lips and takes my tongue, and fuck, my cock aches. She gets it going every time.

"I don't want you to go," she rasps when I pull back.

"I know baby, but I gotta. I'll only be a day or two."

She smiles. "I guess it's me and my hand then."

I growl at her, and she giggles.

"Don't you touch that sweet pussy until I'm home, you hear me?"

She grins up at me. "Yes boss."

"Behave. I'll call you when I get there yeah?"

"Yeah," she whispers.

I kiss her again, and when I pull back, my heart is pounding. Fuck, I hate this. I fuckin' hate it. If it goes wrong...no, I can't fuckin' think like that. I will come home to her, and everything will be fine.

I open my mouth and my voice comes out far scratchier than I would usually like. "I love you, Tom Cat. Yeah?"

She beams at me. "Yeah, right back at you, hot stuff."

I grin, and plant another kiss on her lips.

"Later, Tom Cat."

She gives me a weak wave, and I turn and walk out. Fuck, I hope this goes to plan, because if it doesn't, we're fucked. Royally.

~*~*~*~

PRESENT – CIARA

"Hey Addi, you want to come over for pizza tonight?" I say, skipping into the bar a few hours after Spike left.

That's when I see Addi. She's sitting behind the bar, her face a mass of emotions, and she's twiddling her fingers together so quickly she looks like a mad woman. I rush over, concerned, and stop in front of her. "Hey, are you okay?"

She looks up at me, her eyes glassy. "What? Yeah, sorry."

"Addi, what's wrong?"

She bursts out crying, and I know right away that something bad is going down. Addi doesn't just cry for no reason. She's not the crying type. I rush around the bar and kneel in front of her, feeling my heart beginning to thump. I take her hands, and I try to soothe her as much as possible. Maybe her and Cade had a fight right before he left, or perhaps Jackson.

"Tell me what's wrong?" I say gently.

"I'm not supposed to."

She's sobbing heavily now, and my heart begins to thump so fast I can hardly hear myself think. I know what's coming, somewhere deep down, I know what's coming but I ask anyway. "Is it Spike?"

She nods, and looks up, finally cracking. "The ride they went on. It isn't an annual run, it's to kill Hogan."

I stumble backwards, her words hitting me like a blow to the head. I land on my ass, and my world spins. Spike has gone to kill Hogan. Oh god, Spike has gone to kill Hogan. I tremble violently, and my stomach lurches. No, this can't be happening, Spike can't do this. Not now. Not ever. My fear turns into frenzy, and I leap to my feet.

"Where are they? I can stop him."

"It's too late," Addi croaks. "They're gone."

"There has to be a way!" I scream at her. "Addison, they will get killed."

She starts to cry again, and I curse loudly. Keep calm, Ciara. Keep calm. I kneel in front of her again, trying to steady my panting. "Addi, honey, please…tell me there is a way for us to find them?"

She lifts her eyes, and peers out the front door. "Two of the boys were following late, and they're still here. They're about to ride."

I get to my feet quickly and I turn, skidding around the bar. Addison calls my name, and I spin around, trembling "Addi, don't try and stop me. Nothing you can say right now will stop me from following them. I need to stop those guys, I don't care what I have to do."

She nods, understanding, then she reaches under the bar and pulls out a gun. She stretches her hand out, and I walk over, taking it from her. We stare at each other a long moment, then she pulls me into her arms.

"I know I can't stop you, Ciara, but please...think before you act."

"I promise," I whisper, pulling back and tucking the gun into my pants. "Thank you."

I turn and rush out the front door, and over to my car. I peer around the compound, until I see the two guys just starting up their bikes. God, I was just in time. A minute or two later, and I'd be done for.

I slide into my car and I turn it on. I don't have a second to think about what I'm doing—I just do.

When the bikes pull out of the compound I follow them. I really hope I don't lose them, or worse, that they realize they are being followed. I have to get to Spike before he gets to Hogan, there's just no other option. I can't let anything happen to him.

If he dies, I'll never recover.

I have to get there.

CHAPTER 20

PRESENT – CIARA

Hogan's compound is huge, and when I say huge, I mean it. There are six large sheds, two houses, a large building and a mass amount of Harley-Davidsons lined up. God, Spike is putting himself into a death trap.

I spent the entire day following the two bikers, and when they caught up to Spike's group, I followed them to a long, empty dirt road that has a perfect view of Hogan's compound without them being seen or heard easily.

I parked my car far down the road after they went down it, so they wouldn't see it. Then I got out and I walked the rest of the way. Now I'm crouched behind a mass of trees, peering over at the compound. Spike, Cade, Jackson and Granger are all huddled together in a group, talking frantically amongst themselves.

There's also a man in a car. He's only young, but he's wearing Jackson's colors, so I guess he's one of Jackson's guys. He's on the phone, talking quickly. I watch as Spike turns, and waves at the man in the car. He gets out, and joins the group. I can't hear what they're saying, and if I move closer, they'll see me. I have to pick the right moment to show myself - if I don't, I could get us all killed.

My heart is thumping, and sweat is running down my face. I'm so terrified, my entire body tingles with fear. I wipe my hand over my face as I watch them talking to the strange man, and pointing to the compound and the car. The man nods, listening, and then he turns and gets back into the vehicle.

Then the car moves. I get out of my crouching position to see where it's going. I realize when it pulls out onto the road, and then turns, that it's going to Hogan's lot. Oh. My. God. They're sending someone in? That's so dangerous, so incredibly dangerous. I get on my tiptoes, trying to see more, and I end up falling backwards. I land with a loud crash into a bush behind me. I curse and squirm, trying to get up. It takes me a few minutes, and when I look up, I see four bikers standing and pointing guns down at me. I squeal, and suddenly I'm being hurled up and Spike's hand is clamped over my mouth.

"What the motherfuck are you doing here?" he snarls into my ear.

He lets my hand go, and I shove at his chest. "You lied to me!"

"You fuckin' followed me. Ciara, what the fuck? Do you have any idea how dangerous this is?"

"You could be killed! You didn't think that would matter to me?"

"You fuckin' stupid girl," he growls, his body heaving. "You don't fuckin' mess with a bikers business. You need to get the fuck out of here, right now."

"No," I cry.

"Prez, she needs to fuckin' leave, now," Granger hisses. "Fuck, she's goin' to get us killed."

"Fuckin' right she does," Cade adds. "Ciara, what the fuck were you thinkin'? Biker business is just that, and it ain't none of yours...you need to go."

"You guys can't do this, you can't..."

I'm cut off, because I hear a mass amount of bullets being fired. I yelp, and Spike spins around. All four of them begin running toward their viewing point, and I follow. When I look down, I see a very dead man on the ground. It takes me a moment to realize who that man is. It's the guy they just sent in. Suddenly, the bikers around him look up to where we are standing. Spike pulls everyone back, cursing and swearing. He drives his fist into a nearby tree, then he spins to the group. "He fuckin' knows. He didn't even get in. That fucker knew!"

"We gotta go, Prez. Like now," Granger says, his voice full of panic.

"Get fuckin' Ciara outta here, now!" Spike growls, pulling out his keys.

Granger takes hold of me, and begins pulling me backwards. I struggle in his grip, but my protest is cut off when an almighty boom rocks us. I scream, but no one can hear it, because the sound is deafening. Little bits of god knows what are flying everywhere, and I'm on the ground before I know what's happening. I feel blood trickling down my head, and panic rises in my chest. Oh god, Spike!

Granger releases his hold on me for a second to try and roll, and I scramble out of his arms, crawling toward the bikes. I see Spike, Cade and Jackson on the ground, but all of them are okay. They're bleeding a little from bits that were flying round, but they're ok.

I'm about to call out to Spike, when I see what's happened. Half of Hogan's compound is in a heap - I mean, it's literally in a heap. What was once buildings, is now burning masses that are crumbling to the ground. The car that Cade's guy drove in with just blew up. It's now sitting there, nothing more than a crispy shell.

People are running around frantically, Harleys are roaring to life, and women are screaming. I feel my heart leap into my throat, and I feel sick. Oh god, they blew up the compound. That was the plan all along?

"Was he in there?" Spike hisses to Cade.

"Yeah, he was, we fuckin' checked."

"Good, let's fuckin' ride."

Spike spins around to see me, and his eyes flare. "Ciara, fuck, what the hell!"

"Y-y-y-y-you…you…you…"

"She's in shock, fuck. Where's Granger?" Jackson barks.

"We got no time to fuck around, we gotta go," Cade says.

"You two go, find Granger. I'll get Ciara on the bike. We're outta here."

Spike takes my hand and tugs, and the other two disappear through the fine cloud of smoke that is slowly filling the spaces between the trees. I can still hear screaming, and god, it's a sound I'll never forget. Spike wraps his arms around me, holding me tightly, as he hurries us toward his bike.

Then everything changes. It's funny how quickly something can go from bad to worse. It happens so fast you barely get a chance to blink, let alone think.

I didn't get a chance to think, I didn't even get a chance to say I was sorry—nothing could be done about what happened next. Spike is moving me, and then suddenly bullets are being fired. It takes me a moment, a stupid moment, to realize what those bullets are hitting.

239

Spike's body jerks with each bullet, almost like he's having a fit. He manages to spin himself, and shield me. He finds a moment to protect me, yet I couldn't find a moment to do the same. His entire body jerks, and jerks, and jerks, as bullets are fired into his torso. His eyes roll back, his mouth is suddenly open and he's making a gagging, strangled sound. I know I'm screaming; yet everything seems to happen in slow motion.

Spike's body slides down mine, and drops to the floor. Blood is pouring from the wounds, and it's covering his entire body. I look up, my eyes hazy, to see a man standing about fifty meters away, loading his gun.

I do the only thing I can think of. I pull the gun from my pants and I aim it at him. I pull the trigger.

Blood splatters fill the air for a second, and then he slumps to the ground. I just killed someone, and yet it doesn't even register. The only thing that registers is the bleeding form in front of me. I drop to my knees, and I crawl over, strangled, broken sounds sliding from my throat.

I don't know how I move from one thing to the next, I just know that by the time Cade and Jackson come back, I am pumping Spike's chest over and over. I'm covered in blood, from head to toe. Spike is gurgling, blood bubbling from his mouth. I'm pumping and pumping, begging, pleading, screaming, choking.

"Fuck, fuck." I hear, but I don't know who says it. "Get her outta here, now."

Someone tries to touch me, but I slap their hand away. I can't let him go. If I let him go, he'll die. There's so much blood. God, it's everywhere. He's making strange sounds, his eyes are open, but he's not focused on anything. If I stop, I lose him. I can't stop. I have to help him. I have to save him. Spike, oh god, please wake up.

"Spike, please," I hear myself rasp. "Baby please, you're going to be okay. Spike, wake up. Spike, please don't close your eyes."

"We gotta get out, now. Get Spike."

"Ciara." I think that's Jackson. "You gotta move."

"Spike," I wail, as his body begins jerking, like he's having a fit. Blood begins to splutter from his mouth as he coughs and chokes, and his eyes continue rolling. It's without a doubt the scariest thing I have ever encountered in my entire life. I start screaming again, loudly, desperately, and my hands begin pumping harder and harder on his chest. "SPIKE!"

"Ciara, we gotta move!"

Frantic voices. Screaming. Gun shots. Bikes. I can't pinpoint one noise, they're all haunting my mind. I clutch Spike's shirt and I keep pumping, my fingers curled in the blood-soaked cotton, his blood pooling and flowing like a tap.

"I'm sorry, Ciara."

It's the last thing I hear, before something hard hits me over the head.

After that everything goes black. But darkness doesn't remove pain, it just numbs it...

For a moment at least.

CHAPTER 21

PRESENT – CIARA

"Ciara, hey…"

I hear the voice and I open my eyes, blinking rapidly to try and bring my vision back. I see Addison, and my heart fills with relief. That lasts a split second. When I remember why I am here, I jerk up in the bed and cry out loudly. "SPIKE!"

Addison grips my shoulders, trying to push me back down. "Hey, you need to lie down. Honey, you hurt your head."

"Spike, where is he?" I wail. "Addison, where is he?"

She looks down at me, her eyes filled with a pain I never wanted to see. No, no…NO.

"No!" I scream. "No, Addi, no!"

She pulls me into her arms. "He's alive, hey, shhhh. It doesn't look good, though. I'm so sorry, but the doctors don't know if he'll survive."

My screaming intensifies, and Addi just sits there, holding me. No. This can't be happening. It can't be. Spike is all I have. He's everything. I'm in love with him. He's the reason I breathe. No, this can't happen.

"Hey, sugar."

I hear Cade's soft voice, and I open my tear-filled eyes to see him standing at the side of the bed, looking down at us.

"Cade," I wail. "Cade, he can't leave me."

Cade swallows, and his eyes grow glassy. "I'm sorry, Tom Cat."

"It's my fault, it's all my fault."

He grips my chin, his face determined. "No, it's not. It went wrong. It happens. It ain't on you."

I sob even harder, and Cade crawls onto the bed beside us. Then we just sit there, the three of us, praying in our own way that a miracle happens, and he makes it through. Something has to happen. He can't die. He just can't.

FOUR HOURS LATER

"Ciara?"

I turn to see a doctor walking into the room. I sit up in bed, but he waves a hand at me. "Sorry, there's no news. I am here to check on you."

"I'm fine," I whisper.

"You had a couple of hard falls; I'd just like to make sure."

He walks over, and I sit still while he goes over me. I don't even want to move. I just can't be bothered. Everything inside me feels like it's stopped. When he's done, he pulls back.

"You're ok to go whenever you need. Just keep an eye on that bump on your head. If you get any severe headaches, come back. I know you're waiting for Danny, so feel free to stay in this room while you do."

"Thank you," I whisper.

He nods, and then leaves. Cade walks into the room a moment later, holding two cups of coffee. His face is broken, and his large body is slumping slightly, but he's trying to keep it together.

"Any news?" he asks.

"No, nothing."

I take the hot coffee he hands me, and I take a sip. I can't taste it, I can't even feel its heat. I'm numb. I've been sitting, staring at the wall for the past three hours, just hoping something happens. I can't grieve. I can't have hope. I just don't know which way to lean.

"We'll know soon," Cade assures me.

I hope so.

ANOTHER FOUR HOURS LATER.

"Are you Danny's next of kin?"

I turn in my chair to see a doctor standing at the door. I stand quickly, dropping the magazine that was on my lap that I wasn't actually reading. I rush over, my body feeling numb. I reach him, and my eyes frantically search his expression to see if I can see the "I'm sorry, he's dead" look.

"I am," I croak.

He nods. "He's out of surgery. We removed all the bullets. There were six of them, but he was lucky. I don't know how, and I've never seen someone so lucky in my life, but none of those bullets didn't hit anything important. He had four in his lower back, and two on the right side of his body. If they had hit the left side, he would be dead. There was some damage to his stomach, but we repaired it. He lost a lot of blood, and it was touch and go for a minute there, but he came out of it. He's in intensive care, and the next twenty-four hours are crucial, but he's stable."

I don't hear anything past the "he's out of surgery." I just feel my legs wobble, and my entire body begins to shake. The doctor reaches out and grips my arm. "Are you okay, miss?"

"Can I see him?" I whisper.

He nods. "One at a time, for now."

He leads me out of the room and down the hall. I don't even think to tell the others: all I can think about is Spike.

We get to a dark room, and I can hear the beeping of the machines. I walk in, and there he is, tubes everywhere, machines everywhere, but I can see the steady rising and falling of his chest, and that's enough for me.

Tears slide down my cheeks as I walk closer. I can't hear anything else around me. I can't see anything but him. I stop beside his bed, and reach down, gripping his hand and pulling it into mine. Nurses flutter around, but I don't notice them. I just stare at him. My life.

"I'm here," I whisper to him. "Baby, I'm here."

I take a seat beside him, and I hold onto his hand for hours. The others come in one at a time, hug me, sit with him, and then they leave. I don't move. My legs are numb, my body hurts, but I sit there until his eyes begin to flutter open.

I leap to my feet, squeezing his hand and gently stroking his hair. He blinks, and stares at me blankly for a good, solid few minutes. Then he opens his mouth, and he rasps, "Ciara?"

Oh God.

I break down, sobbing like a child and clutching his hand. "I'm here, baby, it's okay. You're going to be okay."

He blinks a few times, and then he lets his eyes scan the room. "Where…"

"You're in the hospital, you got shot. Do you remember?"

He looks hazy, so I press the nurse button. Two of them come in a moment later, and when they see he's awake, the practically shove me out of the way to check him over. I step out of the room, knowing the others will want to know. I find them in the waiting room, tired and worn, looking like shit.

"He's awake," I say, my voice hoarse.

They all sigh with relief.

"You guys go home, I'm ok here."

Addison stands, and walks over. She takes me into her arms and holds me tightly. "It's okay. We're all going to be just fine now."

I nod, hugging her tightly, then I pull back and hug the rest of them, even Granger.

"You let us know when we can come back and see him, yeah?" he says to me.

"Yeah," I nod. "I promise."

They all leave, and I head back to Spike's room. When I get in, the nurses are just leaving, and he's sitting up slightly in the bed. His eyes fall on me, and he forces a weak smile. I walk in, swallowing down my tears. I stop at his bed, and I take his hand.

"Spike, I'm so sorry."

He shakes his head weakly. "Ain't your fault, Ciara."

"It is my fault. I showed up."

"If you didn't show up, I might be dead. That would have gone how it went," he croaks. "Wouldn't have mattered if you were there or you weren't."

"I was so scared," I say, and the tears finally slide down my cheeks.

"I know," he rasps, reaching for my hand.

"I thought you were dead."

"Hey," he whispers. "I'm okay."

I gently climb onto the bed next to him, and I stroke my fingertips over his hand. I can't hold him, but I can lie with him.

"We're going to be okay, aren't we? Are they going to come after us?"

He's quiet a long moment, his breathing steady.

"I don't know. I really don't know."

Neither do I, and that's the scary thing. We walked away from something, but we left it incomplete. I don't think it's over.

I think it's far from.

I think we may have started a war.

~*~*~*~

PRESENT - SPIKE

"Baby," I whisper, shaking Ciara's shoulders. "You should go."

She groans beside me, and her eyes flutter open to stare up at me. She has a bruised face, and her eyes are bloodshot. I feel my heart clench for her, and it fuckin' hurts. She reaches up, sliding her fingers over my face. I know she doesn't want to leave, but I can see how tired she is. She thought I was dead. The look on her face when she came in my room when I woke up was something I'll never forget. Even now, she looks like she's going to burst out into a fit of tears.

"I don't want to leave you," she croaks.

I reach up, touching the soft skin on her cheek. "You need to leave, and get some rest."

"I know, but it doesn't mean I want to."

"Hey you two!"

We both turn to see Cade and Addison standing at the door. Addi smiles, walking over and stopping by my bed. She stares down at me, then reaches out and puts her hand on my shoulder.

"We've been over this before, if you wanted my attention you just had to ask…"

I laugh weakly, and my entire body feels like someone is beating me as I do. Everything hurts.

"Precious, always makin' me smile."

She smiles down at me, but even I can see she's about to burst into a fit of tears.

"Don't you start fuckin' cryin' too," I rasp.

She nods, clenching her jaw. "You have grown on us, you know?"

I smile, weakly. "I know, precious."

Cade is still standing at the door, his face blank. I look up at him, and I know he's emotional. It's written all over him, even though he's trying not to show it.

"Hey precious," I say to Addi. "Would you take my girl home?"

Addi nods, "Of course, come on honey."

Ciara turns to me, her eyes hurting. "Are you sure?"

I grip her, pulling her down for a soft kiss. "Yeah, go on, I'll call you when I've had some rest, yeah?"

She nods, stroking her fingers across my cheek. "I love you."

"Yeah, I know baby. I love you, too."

I watch the two girls leave the room, and then I turn my eyes to Cade. He's still watching me. Fuck. I'm tired of this. I've hated him for so long, so fuckin' long, and when I was dyin' on the ground I realized how quickly life can end. It wasn't his fault Cheyenne died, no, it was my fuckin' fault. He was only doing what he thought best at the time. I meet his gaze, and force a smile. "You know me, always trying to be the life of the party."

He laughs hoarsely, and walks into the room, stopping at my bed. "You fuckin' scared me, seein' you goin' down…"

I nod. "Yeah, sorry about that."

He hesitates for a moment, then he rasps, "Spike, I know things between us have been fucked up, but I don't wanna spend the rest of my life not bein' your friend. You've always been my go to, always been my wingman. I know we've been getting along for the sake of taking Hogan down, but I'm fuckin' tired of the pretend. You know I'm fuckin' sorry for what happened that day, and if I could take it back, I would."

"It wasn't your fault," I rasp, feeling my voice shake. Fuck, here it comes. I don't wanna show pain in front of him, but it ain't backin' down. "It was mine. I was just lookin' for someone to blame, because I wasn't about to face that I put her in that position. It's on me, Cade."

Cade nods, his eyes glassy. Fuck. *Fuck.*

"Can we move past this? Can we try and be friends? 'Coz fuck, Spike, I don't ever wanna see you where you were yesterday, and not have told you I fuckin' love you."

That's it for me. I turn my head away, my chest heaving with emotion. Fuckin' pussy, *suck it up.* Cade puts a hand on my shoulder, and I turn to face him again. "You fuckin' scared me, do you hear me? You fuckin' scared me."

A single, lone tear slides down my cheek. "I thought I was fuckin' dead, Cade. I thought it was fuckin' done. Never been so fuckin' scared that I wouldn't wake up again."

My body shakes, and Cade leans forward, gripping my head and bringing it to his gut. He wraps both arms around it, and he just holds me there. It's a very brutal hug, and I feel like a fuckin' girl, but fuck, I can't stop my body shaking. I can't stop it no matter how

250

hard I try. I nearly died. I nearly fuckin' died. I was a fuckin' idiot, and I nearly left everybody broken, *again*.

"You fuckin' do that to me again, I'll put you on your ass," Cade chokes from above me.

We stay in that position for a while, and then Cade lets me go. He takes a deep breath to control his emotions. I slowly stop trembling, and manage to crush the fear back down where it came from. I can't live with it. I won't let anything else destroy me. I glance up at Cade, and I know he deserves my forgiveness. I know he deserves it more than anyone. I reach out my hand and he looks down at it.

"I know I fucked up, buddy. I treated you like a dog, and it wasn't on you. I can't take back what I did, but I can ask for us to move on and be friends again. So, what do you say? Friends?"

Cade reaches over, slapping his hand into mine, and gently pulling me back into his fuckin' gut. Soft ass.

"You stupid fuckin' idiot, we never stopped bein' friends."

I snort.

He laughs.

And just like that, the past is forgotten.

EPILOGUE

SIX WEEKS LATER

"God, Spike," I cry as he thrusts in and out of my body, plunging deep.

"Baby, no fuckin' sex for four weeks, ain't no way in shit I am stoppin' this anytime soon."

His hands are in my hair, and I'm bent over the empty bar at the Hell's Knights compound. It's risky, anyone could walk in, but we don't care. We've been fucking like rabbits for the past two weeks. Before that, Spike had to take it easy, and that meant no sex. He suffered too, every damn day. Poor thing.

"I don't want you to stop," I mewl, pushing my ass into his pelvis.

He wraps a hand around my belly, and gently strokes as he thrusts his cock in and out. "Gotta go easy, baby, can't hurt you."

I don't listen; I'm too close to coming. I grip the bar harder, and feel myself building higher and higher as he slams into me harder and harder. I come a moment later, losing my mind for a split second. I cry out, and Spike follows suit, pumping his release into me and growling loudly. I release one hand, and find my clit, rubbing every shudder from my body. Spike's growling subsides, and gently he pulls out of me, pulling me up into a standing position with him. He runs his hands over my dress, dropping it back down, and then he pulls up his jeans. He keeps his chest pressed to my back, as he runs his hands down my belly.

"You okay in there, junior?"

I giggle.

Two weeks after Spike's surgery, I found out I was, in fact, pregnant. All along, I had been carrying his child. We found out just after he got home from hospital, and surprisingly, he was thrilled. Something about a near death experience making him pull his head out of his ass.

"She's fine," I smile, leaning my head back into his shoulder.

"Or he."

"Oh no, totally a she."

He grunts. "More females."

I spin around, gripping his hair and bringing his lips down over mine. "We're not so bad."

"No, babe, you ain't."

I grin up at him, and he runs a finger down over my nose and stops at my lips. "You know, I'm still punishing you for disobeying me?" he growls.

"How long are you going to punish me?" I ask innocently, batting my eyelashes at him.

"Oh, for fuckin' months, baby."

I giggle, and he grips my hair, his eyes flaring with lust.

"Goin' to put my hand to your ass many more times before I'm through…"

I lean up, and bite his lower lip. "So long as you're deep inside me while you're doing it, I don't mind."

"Fuck, Tom Cat, you're makin' me hard again."

I pull back, giggling. "You're always hard."

He snorts. "I'll show you hard in a minute."

I beam up at him, and then suddenly I remember something I needed to give him. My eyes widen, and a big smile stretches across my face.

"What are you smilin' like that for?" he grins.

"Wait here."

He raises his brows as I turn and rush to my purse; I gather what I need out of it and hurry back. He's still standing, watching me with a curious expression. I step forward, feeling my heart beginning to pound.

"Close your eyes."

"Seriously?" he mumbles.

"Yes, seriously, now do it."

He closes his eyes with a sigh, and I reach for his hand. He raises it up, and I gently secure a bracelet around his wrist. My chest tightens as I look down at it, remembering the day I gave it to him, and also the day he gave it back to me. I hurt him, he hurt me, but finally we've managed to make it through. He opens his eyes and stares down at the bracelet on his wrist, and then he looks up and stares into mine with an expression loaded with emotion.

"I gave this to you a long time ago, promising that I would always be there for you. I wasn't there for you when I should have been, and I let my hurt get in the way. You gave this back to me, because I hurt you, and now I'm returning it. I want you to know I'll always be here for you, Spike. No matter what happens in life, I will never abandon you again. That's my promise to you."

His eyes scan my face. "Fuck, Tom Cat...you're makin' my heart do crazy things."

I step up closer to him. "You've been making my heart do crazy things for a long time now, I'm just glad I finally get to share it with you."

He smiles down at me, his eyes full of love. "Fuckin' love you, you know that, yeah?"

I beam. "Yeah, I know that."

"Just makin' sure you know, now and for the rest of your life."

I grip his jaw, and pull his face to mine, crushing our lips together. He kisses me with ferocity, and I return it, groaning and tangling my fingers in his shirt. We stay like that for a long while, just kissing, loving and showing each other everything we've so desperately wanted to show for years. When we pull apart, we're both smiling, both happy, both content. We made a promise to each other, here and now, but this time...

This time we're going to keep it.

~*~*~*~*

After we get over kissing and enjoying each other, Spike and I finally turn and leave the bar. We walk into the yard to find everyone else, and that's when I see Addison, on her knees, arms around...is that a girl? Spike and I glance at each other, and rush over. Addi is soothing a pretty, dark haired girl, who is sobbing like a small, broken child. When she looks up, I gasp. Her face is busted up, and she's got blood running down her face. Some of it has dried, other parts are still fresh. Her eyes, I think they are brown, are bloodshot and frantic.

"Can you tell me your name?" Addi asks the girl.

I hear boots crunching, and look up to see Jackson and Cade rushing out. "What's goin' on?" Jackson asks, kneeling down. "Who is this Addi?"

Addi looks at him. "I don't know, she just walked in."

The girl looks up, and she begins to cry again. "Please," she croaks. "Please don't send me back out there. He's looking for me."

"Who?" Jackson asks.

"M-m-my father. He'll kill me. Please. I have nowhere to go. He tried to kill me, and I ran away. I can't go back."

"How did she stumble in here?" I ask Addi quietly.

"She just walked in, I don't know, she just kind of…appeared."

Odd. Why would anyone walk into a biker's lot? Maybe she's out of it.

"What do we do?" I ask, looking at Jackson.

"What's your name?" he asks the girl, his eyes travelling over her body looking for more injury. They seem to soften a touch. Jackson has a soft spot for people in need of help.

"I…I…It's Serenity."

"Where are you from, darlin'?" he asks her gently.

"I don't know," she croaks, tears welling in her eyes. "I just ran away…"

"All right, all right," he soothes. "It's fine. We're gonna get you all cleaned up, yeah? My daughter here is goin' to take good care of you."

Addi helps the girl to her feet, and I see she's tiny. I mean, like a pixie. That's kind of what she reminds me of. We watch as Addi takes her inside the compound, then we turn to Jackson.

"How do you think she got in here?" Cade asks, still watching Addi.

"Not sure, looks like she's beaten pretty bad," Jackson says.

"She looks like she hasn't seen food in weeks," Spike adds.

"No, whatever she's runnin' from, it's fucked up. She could be more trouble than she's worth."

"You can't send her back out onto the street," I say, watching as Addi disappears into the house. "She looks like she's got nobody."

"Can't keep her here," Jackson says. "Don't know her, and we're an MC club."

"You kept me here," I protest.

He gives me a look. "You knew Cade, you were like family. That girl is a stranger."

"She looks like she's got no one else. Can't we help her out, at least until she finds somewhere to go?"

Jackson sighs, but I know he's given in to me. He is too soft. "You fuckin' women. Fine, she can stay with one of you until you find out more about her, but she ain't stayin' here."

I beam at him, then spin to Spike. "I'm going to see if Addi needs help."

He grins down at me.

"What?" I say.

"You, you're fuckin' sweet, you know that?"

I flush, and lean up on my tiptoes and press my lips to his. "I love you, Danny."

He grunts, and then flashes me a grin. "Back at ya, Tom Cat."

I smile at the group once more, and then I spin around and rush inside. When I get in, Addi is at the sink in the kitchen, washing some cloths for the mystery girls face. I walk over to the girl sitting at the table. She looks tiny in the seat, and she looks beat up, but she's showing absolutely no fear. I know it's strange that I would notice this, but it sparks something inside me. No one, especially not women, should be able to walk into a bikers lot and not feel any fear at all. I just can't understand it. I tilt my head to the side, and watch her scan the room. She's taking everything in, her eyes narrowing. She turns and looks at me, and instantly puts her broken expression back in place.

I can't put my finger on it.

But there's just something not quite right here.

This girl has a story, and whatever that story is…

It ain't pretty.

~*THE END*~

I know you want to beat me right now, but I have to leave Serenity for Jackson's story, Release date TBA!!!

If you liked this book, or even if you didn't, I'd love a review. They all help!! Thank you so much for reading.

Please don't forget to like my Facebook page if you want to keep updated with my work. Xx

Author Bella Jewel

CPSIA information can be obtained
at www.ICGtesting.com
Printed in the USA
LVOW08s0809020217
522985LV00002B/130/P